Geek Cutes

Xine Fury

Geek Cutes
Copyright © 2023 by Xine Fury

ISBN: 978-1-967029-05-1

Geek Cutes

Contents

Dungeon Therapy

March 2020

"Wow, who's she?" I didn't mean to ask it out loud. The woman was in her mid-twenties, and dressed like she made a living turning dalmatians into coats. She wore a white jacket and skirt, with black stockings and gloves, and a matching wide-brimmed hat. Her jacket's high collar obscured most of her face. Even though we were indoors, she wore a huge pair of black sunglasses, reminding me of Holly Golightly.

My friends and I sat in the back room of the gaming store, at one of six tables running role-playing campaigns. From my vantage point, I saw the woman pick up a package of dice and a starter set for Blaggards & Blades.

"She comes in now and then," said the guy next to me. I think his name was Mark. I got the feeling he'd been wanting to hit on me, but couldn't find the words. Either he hadn't noticed the pride bracelet I was wearing, or he didn't recognize the colors of the lesbian flag. "I think she lives up in the hills," he added.

That meant she was rich. The "hills" were actually mountains, and only the richest people in the area owned property up there. The hills were full of log mansions, wedding chapels, and honeymoon chalets. Down here in the valley, we work for a living, mostly catering to the plethora of tourists and hikers who swarm through every day.

While she was dressed to the nines, the customer didn't walk with that air of haughty perfection I would have expected. And I repeat, she was in a games store, buying a copy of Blaggards & Blades. She couldn't have looked more out of place, unless maybe she stopped for lunch at Bubba's Wings on the way home. Try as I might, I couldn't picture this woman playing B&B. Maybe she was buying it for a nephew or something.

As she turned to put her things on the counter, I saw the left side of her head for the first time. Though her face was approximately ninety percent sunglasses, I spotted some dark bruises on her cheek and chin. My first thought was, *That bastard. I'll kill him.* I didn't know who I planning to kill, but probably an abusive husband or boyfriend. Sure, maybe she'd just been in a car wreck or something, but she was obviously dressed to hide the bruises as much as possible. In my experience, women who hid bruises were protecting someone, usually someone who didn't deserve protection.

I nearly stood up. I wanted to march over and demand to know the guy's name. I wanted to convince her – somehow – that she was too good for him, that she deserved someone better, someone like… me? My own thoughts surprised me. I suppose she was attractive, but definitely not my type. And did she even like girls?

While I wrestled with this inexplicable attraction, she paid and left. I wanted to run out after her, and just talk to her. I didn't know what I wanted to say, I just wanted to know what her voice sounded like. I wanted to know if the game she'd bought was for herself. The truth was, I just didn't want her to drive off into the sunset, without getting the chance to know more about her.

I was still debating when the store manager walked into the back room. "Pack it up, everybody, the store's closing early!"

There were some groans and complaints as everyone started putting away their gaming paraphernalia - books, dice, miniatures, maps, pencils, and so on. One of the GMs, a blond guy who worked at the store part-time, approached the manager and asked what was going on. I packed my backpack extra slowly, one ear on their conversation.

"It's that COVID thing," the manager said. "The whole town's about to be on lockdown."

"But what about my hours?" the blond guy asked.

"All I know is that all the stores are closing," the manager told him. "They're probably just being paranoid. I bet it all blows over in a week or two."

"A week or two?" blondie whined. "How am I supposed to buy groceries if I miss two weeks of work?" From what I knew about the blond guy, he lived with his parents, and by "groceries" he probably meant weed.

"I don't know," the manager said. "Just go home, listen to the news, and hope for the best."

I finished packing up my things and went home.

I was pretty lucky, all things considered. I did line work for the Department of Power, and as an essential service, my job was barely affected at all. If anything work was easier, because the empty streets made it quicker to get around town.

Still, I missed throwing dice on the weekends. I'm not into video games, so I couldn't just scratch that itch playing "Endless Fantasy 14" or whatever. I missed the camaraderie, the stories, the satisfaction of rolling a crit... heck, I even missed the math.

The game store had an online message board, which was currently flooded with customers asking, "When are you going to be open again?" But a few of the users had started organizing online games, which used various chat programs. I'm not really a computer person, but I thought I'd give it a go.

I ended up in a group that played Blaggards & Blades for about six hours every Saturday. I knew a couple of the other players already, from the campaigns I'd played in the store. There was Tyler, who used the screen name "Ty-Ranosaur," and Robert, who went by "BobsGift2Women." Spare me. The other players were Sharon, a.k.a. "TiredMomOf3," and Dorothy, who went by "DotMatrix" online. Finally we had our gamemaster, Brant, who used the super creative screen name, "Brant."

We tried several different programs for playing online, and none of them were perfect. One was better at displaying maps and tokens, but failed on the voice chat aspect. One had really good built-in die rollers, but kept crashing if more than three of us logged on at the same time. We ended up using two programs at once. We ran our campaign in a program called U-Bliette, but we also kept CleerVox running in the background so we could talk to each other. There was a bit of a learning curve at first, especially for Brant, but we helped each other through it.

That took up the first three hours of what we gamers call "Session Zero." Then we discussed whether to play through a published module, or to just wing it. Brant already had an idea on that, a series of published one-shots tied together by a central story arc he'd been working on. We agreed, then discussed house rules and taboo subjects.

We all agreed that there would be no rape in our campaign, or any sort of child torture. Any sexual interactions would be of the "fade to black" variety, which relieved Brant, who didn't want to have to describe that kind of thing. Sharon had a thing about spiders, and almost vetoed their inclusion in the campaign, then changed her mind. "I'll let you know if it gets to be too much," she said.

We discussed whether or not to use video chat, but Dorothy didn't have a camera, and Tyler didn't trust the speed of his internet connection. So we decided voice was enough. Besides, it was that much easier to stay in character if we couldn't see each other's faces.

Next we decided what kind of characters we'd be playing. That asshat in the White House had me wanting to smash things, so I offered to be the tank. I rolled up a dwarf fighter named Bjertha Brawlbaker. Tyler made a human rogue named Shade, Robert made an orc paladin named Veritas Puregood, and Sharon made a tiefling warlock named Skorn Blakthorn.

Dorothy, who insisted we call her her "Dot," told us she was new to the game, though she'd played other RPGs before. She asked us what class we needed to round out the party. Her only request was that she wanted her character to be drop-dead gorgeous. We suggested a half-elf bard, and she named her character Venus Belle.

We still had another hour of playtime scheduled, but Brant didn't want to jump into the campaign without a little more prep time. Instead, we played a couple of test battles to see what the software could do. It wasn't bad. It would never replace the feel of rolling actual dice at a table surrounded by your friends, but it was pretty cool how it did all the math for you. Not ideal, but it would do for now.

After the test fights were over, we still had a good half hour left, so Brant made a suggestion. "To save a little time next week, why don't we go ahead and have your characters meet each other?" We all agreed it sounded like fun.

"All right," Brant said. "You're in a tavern."

"We all meet at a bar?" Sharon asked. "How original."

"My character doesn't drink," Robert said.

"A juice bar, then," Brant said, sounding slightly annoyed.

"Maybe a little anachronous," I said.

"It's a fantasy world," Brant said. "If I say there's juice bars, there's juice bars. And it's in a restaurant. You're the only customers in the place, but you don't know each other. Where are each of you sitting, and what are you doing?" Using the program's drawing tools, he quickly mapped out a layout of the establishment on our screens.

"I'm at the bar," I said. "...asking the waiter if he can sneak a little vodka into my orange juice."

Tyler spoke in a quiet, edgy voice. "I'm at the farthest table from the entrance with my back to the wall, watching the others warily."

"I'm also at the bar, trying to decide which juice looks the most nutritious," Robert said.

"I guess Skorn is at this table," Sharon said, moving her digital token to one of the chairs. "The restaurant seems pretty quiet, so she's studying her spellbook while she eats."

"And you, Venus?" Brant asked.

Dot moved her token to a chair by the fireplace. "I'm sitting in this comfy-looking chair, practicing my harp."

"Nice," I said. "I like music when I drink. What kind of song is it?"

"Um... an old folk tune," Dot said. "I'm singing, too. In Elvish."

"Why don't you give me a performance check," Brant suggested. "Just to see if the others think you're any good."

"Where is that again?" Dot asked.

Brant talked her through making skill checks in the software.

"Twenty-one," Dot said.

"Not bad for the first roll of the campaign," Brant said. "You play quite beautifully."

"Moved by her performance, I walk over and sit at a nearby table," I said.

"Me too," Sharon said.

"Shade stays put," Tyler said. "I never give in to emotion."

"Hey, Rita, does your dwarf have a beard?" Robert asked.

I had to think about it. "Ah, sure. But she keeps it short and carefully trimmed."

"Gross," Tyler said.

"Well, I think it looks very distinguished," Dot said.

"Thank you," I replied. "And I think you have beautiful eyes. Venus does have eyes, right?"

Dot laughed. "I blush and bat my big blue eyes at Bjertha, giving her a demure smile."

"These two babes are totally hitting on each other," Tyler said.

"Was that in character?" I asked.

"Sure, why not," Tyler said.

I'd played with Tyler before, and he often made crude comments. This time, I wanted to nip it in the bud. "In that case," I said, "I stand up and walk over to Shade's table. I pull out my axe, and brandish it menacingly. With fire in my eyes, I say, 'Call me a babe one more time and see what happens.' Then I turn around and head back to the fireplace."

"I draw my dagger," Shade said.

"Well that escalated quickly," Robert mumbled.

Shade continued. "And then I sneak up behind her, and—"

"Wait," Brant interrupted. "As you're standing up from your chair, there's a gust of wind as the front door bursts open. A woman runs into the bar - er, restaurant, and screams. 'Please help me! My baby has been kidnapped by goblins!' Then she collapses. And we'll stop there for the week."

"You got lucky," Tyler said.

I snorted. "One of us did, yeah."

"Same time next Saturday?" Brant asked. We all agreed and logged off.

Tyler didn't show up the following week. Brant had sent him a private message with some constructive criticism, and Tyler had taken it badly. Brant wouldn't give us any more details than that, but we could fill in the gaps. That left the party without a rogue, but that was fine. Dot's bard had a few rogue-ish skills, and Bjertha had no problem disarming traps the old-fashioned way – axe first.

The game went great. We saved the baby from a goblin-infested cave, then met with a prince who gave us a bigger job. Throughout the session, Dot and I flirted a lot – in character, of course, though some of it was borderline. When the session was over, the other players started logging off, but Dot and I stayed connected for a bit.

At one point during the game, she'd quoted one of my favorite movies, an obscure comedy that I was surprised she'd seen. As we got to talking, we discovered we had a lot of favorite movies in common, including some that were almost universally hated. She was fun to talk to, and I wanted to know more about her.

"So, what do you do for a living?" I asked her.

"I'm a stockbroker," she answered.

"Wow," I said. "That's, like, a real job."

She laughed. "I know, right? I'm not even sure how I got into it. I've just always had a thing for numbers. Maybe that's why I like gaming."

"Has the quarantine hurt your business?"

"Not really," she said. "I already did a lot of my work from home. Most of my clients are virtual."

Something didn't add up. "You work from home, with clients, but your computer doesn't have a camera?"

She didn't answer for a second. "I have one," she finally said. "It stopped working a couple of weeks ago. I just haven't gotten around to buying a new one yet."

It sounded like a lie, but I didn't press it. That was her business. She asked me about my work, and sounded really impressed by it. We chatted for another hour before finally logging off.

I thought about Dot a lot over the following week. I looked up her social media accounts and friended her. She used variations of "Dot" or "DotMatrix" on all her accounts. However, there were no photos of her anywhere. Most of her profile pics used a photo of a ladybug, the same avatar she used on her U-Bliette account. To be fair, I didn't post photos of myself online, either.

I sent Dot a couple of messages over the course of the week, but we both had busy weeks at work, so we didn't get into any deep conversations.

The next session was a lot of fun. We retrieved the prince's missing scepter from a bandit hideout, where we also found a treasure map. We hired a ship to take us to a mysterious island, but we ran out of time before we could do any exploration.

Our party had developed a fun dynamic. Veritas, the paladin, was dour and looked down on anything he deemed blasphemous. He was particularly judgmental of Skorn the warlock, because her powers came from a pact with a demon. The banter between Veritas and Skorn was priceless. Meanwhile, Dot and I might have overdone it a bit with the flirting, because at one point Veritas told us to "get a room already."

Once again, Dot and I were the last ones to log out. By this point we each knew the other was a lesbian, and while that alone didn't mean we were destined for couplehood, we both knew some sparks were brewing. But any time I suggested we meet somewhere, she backed off. She blamed the quarantine, but I suspected she was using it as an excuse.

"I didn't mean like, today," I said. "But once the restrictions are lifted. Or when there's a vaccine."

"I just don't want to make any commitments right now," she said. "We don't know how long this thing's going to last."

I was starting to think she preferred the world on lockdown. I must have put too much pressure on her, because she made up an excuse to log off after that. I sent her a few messages over the week, but her responses weren't very wordy. After the third "thumbs up" acknowledgment, I stopped trying. I was starting to worry that I'd blown it.

* * *

We didn't get to play the following week. Brant sent everyone a message on Friday to let us know he couldn't make it. He had the flu, as did both of his kids, which he found perplexing since none of them had left the house since the lockdown started. He said he must have caught it from the guy who'd delivered his groceries. He said he felt like death itself, but at least it wasn't COVID.

The week after that, Brant felt a lot better. We picked up right where we'd left off. At first, Dot and I were a little standoffish with each other, like we couldn't remember how to interact. But within half an hour, the near-salacious repartee between Bjertha and Venus was in overdrive, and we took turns making the paladin blush. By the end of the session we'd explored more than half the island, and had left a trail of dead monsters in our wake. We still hadn't found the buried treasure, but it was only a matter of time.

As usual, Dot and I were the last to leave. "Good game today," I told her. "Sorry if I made you uncomfortable before."

"You didn't," she said. "Well, you did, but you didn't do anything wrong. I have issues, but they're my issues." I didn't press it. We chatted for a little while longer, then we finally logged off.

We continued to play online for over a year. During that time, Dot and I got very close. We'd spend hours on the phone, talking about everything – our jobs, our hobbies, our celebrity crushes. Sometimes we'd go from flirty to downright lewd. But she still refused to send me a photo. She said she wanted to wait until we could see each other in person, but I got the feeling that was just an excuse.

Milestones passed. COVID tests were made readily available. A vaccine was developed. Everyone in our gaming group got both doses. Mask restrictions were loosened. After one session, Brant made an announcement. "You're pretty close to the final boss. I'd say we have two, maybe three sessions left in the campaign. The game store is talking about reopening soon. I was thinking that when we start the next campaign, we go back to meeting in person."

Everyone seemed gung-ho for the idea except for Dot, who stayed quiet. I waited until after everyone logged off to ask her about it.

"I think I might sit the next campaign out," she said.

"Why?" I asked. "Aren't you having fun?"

"I've got things to catch up on around the house," she said. "I've fallen behind on housework."

I could tell she was lying. "Be straight with me," I said. "Is it because we're meeting in person?"

"I don't want to talk about it," she said.

I didn't press her. We kept talking, but it felt like something was hanging in the air between us.

But half an hour later, we'd both forgotten the awkwardness. We got a little flirty for a while, then serious, then *really* flirty. Somehow we got to talking about movie stars we found attractive. It was a little crass, but we weren't judging the celebrities solely on looks, and we weren't badmouthing any of them. We were just curious as to who got each other's motors running.

We named a few celebrities back and forth, until I mentioned someone she hadn't heard of. I sent her a picture.

"Oh her," Dot said. "Yeah, I could definitely see asking her out for a dinner-and-breakfast."

"I hear she's married to the guy from that vampire movie," I said. "What a waste."

"What do you think about this woman?" she asked, and my tablet dinged.

"Is this a celebrity?" I asked, looking at the picture. It wasn't anyone I recognized. She was in her mid-twenties, with long black hair. She was wearing jeans and a white T-shirt. Half her face was covered in dark purple freckles. In some areas, such as her cheek, the spots were so heavily concentrated that they became one large splotch.

The spots continued on her neck, and down her left arm. In fact, every bit of exposed skin on the left side of her body was covered. Her right side had the occasional freckle, but they were mostly concentrated on the left.

She was still quite beautiful, though. She had a perfect face, with the cheekbones of a model, and I could tell she worked out. She didn't have muscle tone like mine – few women did – but I was sure this woman did yoga or Pilates or something.

Also, there was something familiar about her. I was sure I'd seen her somewhere before, but I couldn't think of any mainstream celebrities with her skin condition. "Is she a musician or something?" I asked.

"She's been known to play guitar," Dot said. "But that doesn't matter. What do you think of her?"

"I don't know her," I said. "If she's a fun person, yeah, sure. I'd love to see how far down those freckles go."

Dot got quiet for a minute.

"What?" I asked.

"You really shouldn't fetishize someone's physical deformity," Dot said.

"Oh," I said. Yeah, I'd been crude. But so had she, at least a couple of times in the past ten minutes. "You're right," I finally said. "That was too far. But you're the one who used the word 'deformity.' Don't you think that's a bit much? That woman is gorgeous. Her freckles just make her unique. You make her sound like Frankenstein's monster or something."

"Hmm," Dot said.

"What?" I asked.

"Nothing," Dot said. "You're just… full of surprises."

I felt like I'd just been tested, but I wasn't sure if I'd passed. Our conversation dwindled after that, and we logged off about ten minutes later.

* * *

It was two AM when I suddenly sat bolt upright in bed, and said out loud, "I'm an idiot."   I grabbed the phone off my nightstand and messaged Dot. "U up?"

The reply came back almost immediately. "No."

"Sorry," I typed. "Will call U tomorrow."

I was about to set the phone down when it started buzzing. A picture of a ladybug filled the screen. "Dot?" I asked, putting the phone to my ear.

"What's up?" she asked.

"I meant what I said. You really are beautiful."

"Ah," she said, yawning. "You figured it out. Good work, detective."

"Is this why you didn't want to go out with me?" I asked. "You were afraid I wouldn't find you attractive? Because I do."

"It was one reason," she said. "It wasn't the only reason."

"What then?"

"I don't want to go out at all," Dot said. "I'm not embarrassed by my freckles. Believe it or not, I like the way I look. I wouldn't call myself Dot if I hated it. But I can't stand how other people react to it. You can build up my self-confidence all day, but that all goes out the window when the staring begins."

"Then we'll start small," I said. "I'll take you hiking. Maybe go on a picnic. We'll stick to secluded areas, until you're more comfortable around people."

"You're not listening," she said. "I'm not uncomfortable around people. I'm uncomfortable with the stares and the double takes."

"Then how about some stay-at-home dates?" I suggested. "I'll go to your place, you'll come to mine..."

"At the same time?" she asked, giggling.

"No, silly," I said. "We can watch movies together, play some games..."

"You make it sound so cozy," Dot said. "But I don't want to tie you down. You're an outdoorsy person. You don't want to be stuck with a girlfriend who can't go out in public."

"Do they really stare that much? Are you sure your mind isn't exaggerating? If you're already self-conscious—"

"Don't do that," she said. "I know what I see. I'm not imagining the double-takes."

"They probably just jump because they saw something they didn't expect. It doesn't mean they're judging you, or think you're hideous. If I saw you, I wouldn't stare, I promise."

"You sure stared before," Dot said.

"Huh?"

"Brown hair, big muscles, sometimes dresses like a lumberjack?"

"That does sound like me," I admitted.

"I knew it! I saw you at the game store."

"Really? I think I'd have noticed if you were... Oh, crap! That was you?"

"Yep," she said. "I did everything I could to cover up my freckles, and you still stared like I was from outer space."

"I didn't see your freckles. I saw what I thought was a bruise on your face, but that's not why I stared. I couldn't look away because you were stunning. I knew from that first look that you were someone special."

"Oh," she said.

I waited for her to say something more, but she didn't, so I kept talking. "People just have to get used to you," I said. "It's a small town, except for the tourists. Once all the locals know what you look like, you'll get a lot fewer reactions. But that's never going to happen if you don't leave the house."

"I've tried that," she said. "And I don't appreciate you explaining my own problems to me. I've lived with this all my life. You've known about it for a couple of hours."

"You're right, I'm sorry," I said. "Can I just make one suggestion, though?"

She still sounded angry, but she listened to my proposal.

* * *

We held the following game at Dot's house. She lived in a chalet a few miles up the mountain road, surrounded by trees.

"What if there's bears?" Robert asked, getting out of the car. We'd all ridden together.

"Don't worry, I'm sure I can outrun you," I said, and he playfully punched my arm.

The house was amazing. It was like a three-story log cabin, each floor surrounded by a wraparound deck. It was built on the side of the slope, and on the far side, the balconies stood high above the forest floor. It looked like it had been built to rent to large groups of tourists, but Dot lived there by herself.

Dot met us at the door. No one jumped or stared, as I'd already shown them her picture. With Dot's permission, of course. She still seemed a little nervous at first, but by the end of the session, she was just as boisterous as any of us.

As the session was wrapping up, I asked her, "What do you think?"

"I could definitely get used to this," she said. Then to everyone, she asked, "Want to have next week's session here too?"

"I'm good with it," Brant said. "Your place is awesome."

Everyone packed up their things and said their goodbyes, heading for Brant's car.

"Rita's going to stay and hang out for a while," Dot told them.

"I am?" I asked, then saw the playful smirk on her face. "I mean, yeah. I am."

"How are you going to get home?" Brant asked.

"I'll drive her home later," Dot said.

And she did. The next day.

Despite Brant's prediction, the campaign ended up taking another four sessions, and we played all of them at Dot's house. When we started the next campaign, Sharon wanted to DM this one. She'd been working on a story that she'd been dying to run. She didn't think it would be a very long campaign, maybe six months at most, and we decided to keep playing at Dot's house.

Another interesting development was the return of Tyler, who had previously left the group after a falling out with Brant. He'd been known to make sexist comments in the past, but he swore he was a different person now. Changed or not, he still rolled up another loner rogue with an edgy backstory.

The next three sessions went by without incident. Tyler's character didn't interact much with the rest of the party, but he still managed to be a valuable asset to the team.

During one session, we'd just been rewarded for returning a lost gem, and we decided to take a short break. Dot got up to use the restroom. While she was gone, Tyler started asking questions about Dot's freckles.

"So how far down do the spots go?" he asked. I was uncomfortably reminded that I'd made a similar comment just a few months earlier. Hearing the words come out of Tyler's mouth, it hit home just how gross it was.

"Dude," I said. "Not cool."

"Oh, come on," Tyler said. "I see the way you two act. I know you've seen her naked. What's she look like? What's *it* look like? Is she spotty down there too?"

"Geez, Tyler!" Robert said.

We all heard a gasp and turned our heads. Dot was standing in the doorway, her mouth open. Without a word, she turned around and walked out of the room.

"You jerk," Sharon said.

"Should I go talk to her?" I asked.

"Maybe give her a minute," Brant said.

Robert started putting his things away. "We should probably wrap it up anyway," he said.

As we packed up our dice and minis, Sharon glared at

Tyler. "You're out of the group," she said. I might have waited until we were all home and informed him by e-mail, but Sharon rarely shied from confrontations.

"What?" Tyler asked, his face turning red. "I was just curious, I didn't mean anything by it."

"If you don't know, we can't help you," Robert said.

"Fine," Tyler grumbled, then reached into his bag. He pulled out a gun.

Robert shrieked and backed away from the table. Brant shouted, "What the fuck?"

Tyler stood up and held the gun on us. "I don't need you people," he said. "I thought you were cool, but you're just like everyone else."

"What are you talking about?" Sharon asked, cringing as the barrel pointed in her direction.

"Tyler, think about this," I said. "Whatever's wrong, this isn't going to fix it."

"None of you ever respected me," Tyler said. "Everything I do is wrong!"

"What's all the shouting?" Dot asked, coming back into the room. She gasped when she saw the gun.

"And it's all your fault!" Tyler shouted, turning toward Dot. He fired, the sound echoing throughout the entire house. Somewhere in the distance, glass broke. Dot crumpled to the floor.

I rushed forward and tackled Tyler from behind. The rest of the group joined in, and we wrestled the gun out of his hand.

Sharon called the police, while Robert and Brant kept Tyler restrained. I ran over to check on Dot.

"I'm okay, I was just scared," she said, getting up. I checked her over for wounds, but she was fine. Tyler had missed her completely.

Before the incident, Tyler had never fired a gun in his life. The bullet had missed Dot by a mile, instead going through the wall and breaking a window in the back of the house. He only spent three months in jail, but none of us ever saw him again. We suspended the game for a couple of weeks, but when we resumed, we kept playing at Dot's place.

"I hope Tyler hasn't made you more agoraphobic," I said one night after the game.

"You won't believe this," she said, "But if anything, I'm less afraid. Tyler was a jerk, but he was a jerk to all women. He tried to make it about me, but if I hadn't been here, sooner or later he would have made a crude joke about you or Sharon. You'd have called him on it, and it would have ended the same way. He was a bomb waiting to go off."

"Well, I'm just glad he was a lousy shot," I said.

"Tell that to my window," Dot said, and we laughed.

"Crit!" Dot shouted. "Thirty-seven damage. Take that, ya big lizard!"

"And that brings him down to… negative twelve," Brant said. "The dragon falls over, shaking the entire room as its massive head hits the stone floor. The treasure is yours for the taking."

"Way to go, Dot!" Sharon said.

Another six months had passed. We all sat around the table, in person, in the back room of the games store. Dot wore a light sleeveless T-shirt, showing off more skin than I'd ever seen her show in public. She looked so happy, and what's more, she looked comfortable.

While Brant wrapped up the session, a customer walked into the store and started browsing. As he walked past the doorway to the back room, he saw Dot. He did a little double-take, then went back to looking at miniatures. Dot chuckled and kept right on celebrating the dragon's defeat.

Watching her beautiful smile, her bright eyes, and the animated way her hands moved as she recounted her victory, it dawned on me just how much she meant to me. A few minutes later, as we stood up to leave, she leaned over to me and whispered, "You were staring again."

"I never want to look at anything else," I said. We left the game store and headed back to her home, together.

Gilded Cage

"And don't come out until you like boys!"

Lindy recoiled from the slamming door. She ran to her window and looked down at the driveway below. Her father was leading Ronnie to the car. The girl walked with the gait of a prisoner being led to the electric chair. Lindy's eyes filled with tears as she watched the car pull out of the driveway. Would she ever see her best friend again? Not if her parents could help it.

Her mom had taken her phone, but Lindy still had her laptop. She flipped it open, hoping to send Ronnie a message. "I'm sorry my parents are like this," she typed. "I promise we'll get through this. I love you." She paused for a few seconds, reconsidering the last three words. They hadn't actually said them yet, and she didn't want to scare Ronnie off. She backspaced it out, then retyped it, twice. *What have I got to lose?* she finally thought.

She clicked send, but a little red exclamation mark appeared next to the message. Lindy looked down at the taskbar, and saw that the wi-fi wasn't connected. She tried to reconnect, but it wouldn't take her password.

Already? she thought. She searched for other wi-fi connections, but the house was pretty isolated.

Lindy sat on her bed and put her face in her hands. It was all too much. Not half an hour ago, Lindy was on cloud nine.

She could still taste Ronnie's vanilla lip gloss. If only they'd locked the door.

She'd always known her parents were homophobic, but her mom's reaction still shocked her. She'd nearly yanked Lindy's arm out of the socket pulling her away from Ronnie. She'd yelled so hard she'd gone hoarse, her religious tirade so impassioned it became gibberish. *How can she believe in a god that wouldn't want me to be happy?* Lindy wondered. *What kind of god would call love a sin?*

She vowed right then and there that she would never grow up to be her parents. She would never follow a religion that taught bigotry as a virtue. And if she ever had kids at all, she would encourage them to be whoever they wanted to be. Unless they wanted to be bigots. Then they'd be grounded for life.

Lindy stood up and looked around her room. As prisons went, it was luxurious. The room had once been the master bedroom, but her mom didn't like climbing all the stairs, so they'd given it to Lindy. The room was huge, with its own bathroom, and plenty of space for all her projects. She took after her father, who was an aerospace engineer. Remote control airplanes and drones, some only half-built, sat on every shelf.

The house had once been a small private airport, but that was decades ago. Her dad still used the runway out back for his vintage biplane. Lindy's room was in the control tower, which was three stories higher than the rest of the house. Huge windows surrounded her on all sides. The view had once made her feel free, like she was living in the clouds.

But today she felt more like a fairytale maiden, locked in a tower by a wicked witch. She tested the door. It really was locked from the outside. She knew there was a latch outside the door, but this was the first time she'd seen it used. *Seriously?* she thought. *This is child abuse.* Some of the windows opened, but not wide enough to climb out. She supposed she could break one, but then what? She didn't think her sheets were long enough to make a rope.

She looked out the window again. Her dad's car was long gone. Ronnie only lived fifteen minutes away. Any minute now she'd be facing her own sentence. And Lindy knew that Ronnie's parents were just as bigoted. *I hope she's okay*, Lindy thought.

She sat back down, cried a little, then screamed at the top of her lungs. Then she stood up, moved to her computer desk, and opened her laptop again. She wanted to write down her feelings while the anger was still fresh. But she couldn't figure out how to start, and just stared at the blank text document. She stood up again and paced around the room. She wanted to break something. She took a model airplane off the shelf and got ready to hurl it at the wall. Then she stopped, sighed, and put it back on the shelf.

She wasn't going to get out of this by throwing a temper tantrum. She was seventeen years old, and a senior in high school. Freedom wasn't that far off. If she played her parents' game until graduation, she could date whoever she wanted in college. But that seemed so far away…

Lindy threw herself face down onto the bed. It was the middle of the day, but she was emotionally exhausted. Soon the tears came again, and she cried herself to sleep.

She woke to the sound of her door closing, and fading footsteps thumping down the metal stairs. The sun had gone down. The lights were off, so she turned on her bedside lamp. Three bags were sitting by her door. Fighting off a headache, she rolled off the bed and stumbled across the room. She flipped on the overhead lights, tried the door again – still locked – then kneeled to examine the bags.

First was a sack from her favorite fast food restaurant. She could smell the aroma of greasy chicken from within. Most days she would have found the smell heavenly, but right now it made her a little nauseous. She pushed it aside and grabbed the second bag. There was a note taped to it, which read "We still love you." Lindy crumpled up the note and tossed it over her shoulder, then opened the bag.

She gasped with indignation when she saw what was inside. It was a child's cell phone. It had four buttons, which could only be programmed by the account holder. The first two were labeled Mom and Dad; the other two weren't yet programmed. *So this is what it's come to,* Lindy thought.

The third bag was a brown paper sack, stapled shut. Lindy picked it up, noting that it felt like it contained several items. She set it on her bed before opening it.

First, there was a package of condoms. Lindy was so incredulous, she almost laughed. "What am I supposed to do with these?" she asked out loud. Even if she liked boys, she wasn't going to meet any locked in this tower. Next, there were four DVDs. As soon as Lindy realized what they were, she shrieked and tossed the whole stack across the room. The nude men on the covers stared back at her from the floor. *Those are going right in the trash,* she thought.

Next there was an unmarked rectangular box, inside a cardboard sheath. She slid off the outer sheath, and her eyes became saucers. *What. The. Fuck.* It was a sex toy, a hyperrealistic phallus with dozens of vibration modes. "Mom has lost her mind," Lindy said, setting the box down. She looked back into the sack. Finally, at the bottom of the bag, there was a bible.

This time she did laugh. She laughed so hard, she was afraid her parents would hear her, even though they lived in a house designed to drown out airplanes. When she no longer had the energy to laugh, she stared off into space, thinking of Ronnie.

"Your *girlfriend* has moved away," Lindy's mom said. She spat the second word, like she'd bitten into a rotten piece of fruit.

"What?" Lindy replied. They sat at a card table in Lindy's room. Her mother had brought her breakfast, and had refused to leave until they talked. Last night's chicken still sat untouched in its bag on the floor.

"After what we told them, they no longer felt California was the best place to raise her. She's going to live with her uncle in Tucson until they decide what to do."

"She hates her uncle," Lindy said. "He never showers and he calls her 'Ronnie-Leigh.' She's going to be miserable."

"She should have thought of that before…" she trailed off, then shook her head. "Lindy," she said, "I… well, your father and I… we want to make you a deal. We'll give you some of your freedom back, if you'll do a couple of things for us."

Lindy stared at her, but didn't say anything. She was still thinking about Ronnie.

"First, we want you to consider going to a local college, and living here."

"What?" Lindy asked, snapping out of her thoughts. "No! That's—"

"Lindy," her mother interrupted. "Go anywhere you like, but you'll have to find a way to pay for it. We'll only pay for your college if you go to one we approve of. Secondly, we want you to try dating some boys."

"Mom, that's—"

"I don't want to hear it. You're young, and today's woke culture has filled your head with silly ideas. No more internet for you, and no more female friends. You'll date who we tell you to date, or you'll stay in your room."

"It's my life!" Lindy shouted.

"And that's why I don't want you to mess it up. You only get one life. I don't want you to look back and realize you wasted your youth, brainwashed by the liberal media. I only want what's best for you."

"Get out of my room," Lindy growled.

Anger flashed in her mother's eyes, but she didn't raise her voice. "I'll let you take some time to think about it," she said, standing. Then she picked up the bag of spoiled chicken and walked out the door, locking the latch behind her.

* * *

A few weeks passed. Her mother drove her to and from school each day, but she spent the rest of her time locked in her room. While at school, Lindy noticed that the teachers seemed to be keeping an extra close eye on her, and she could tell a few students were talking behind her back. The faculty also changed her class schedule so that she no longer went to gym class, and gave her study hall instead.

She wanted to tell her teachers that she was being kept prisoner, but she had the feeling her parents had already spoken to them. It was Lindy's word against theirs, and no one was going to believe her over her parents. Lindy didn't have a lot of friends, but whenever she tried to talk to other girls, the nearest teacher would separate them. "You're here to learn, not socialize," they might say, even if it was between classes.

"There's a boy I want you to go out with," Lindy's mom said. "His name is Sam. His mother thinks he needs to socialize more." They sat at the card table again, eating lunch.

"Mom, I'm really not interested in—"

"I'm not asking you to have sex with him," she said, making Lindy blush. "Just go out, let him buy you dinner and a movie. Even if you don't hit it off, it'll be nice to get out of the house for a change." She said it as if it was Lindy's fault she didn't get out more.

"I just don't—"

"If you do it, I'll let you have your internet back."

"Really?" Lindy perked up, sitting up straighter.

"With some restrictions, of course. I get a list of your passwords, and occasionally your father will go through your computer. You know, your browser history, your chats, make sure you don't have any girlie pictures, that kind of thing. Oh, don't give me that look."

A bit of half-chewed food tumbled out of Lindy's open

mouth, but she was still too shocked to close it.

"Parents, am I right?" Sam said, taking a sip of his cola. "I didn't want to come either. No offense, you seem grice. Nice, I mean. Or great. I just hate being forced into, you know, social situations."

They sat at a picnic table in the park, enjoying a meal of turkey sandwiches and chips. They had the table to themselves, but Lindy's mom sat at another table about thirty feet away, watching them. Presumably so that Lindy didn't run off and start kissing the next girl who walked by.

The thing was, Sam actually was decent company. They shared a few hobbies in common, and liked a lot of the same music. So far they'd been there for nearly an hour, and they hadn't run out of things to talk about. Lindy wasn't about to hop in bed with him, but he was fun to talk to. Or maybe Lindy was just starved for human contact.

Now and then, she'd glance at her mom and make a small "thumbs up" gesture. She hated to be so compliant, but she wanted her internet back. Her mom smiled smugly, as if to say, "See? You were just confused."

When they were done eating, they took turns flying a drone Lindy had brought. Sam had never flown one before, but this drone was designed for beginners, with intuitive controls. Still, he managed to crash it into the trees more than once. They had a great time. For Lindy, it was the happiest she'd been since her kiss with Ronnie.

As they were preparing to leave, Lindy whispered into Sam's ear. "I don't want to make it weird, but would you kiss me? It doesn't mean anything."

"I get it," Sam said, casting a sideways glance at Lindy's mom. Making sure they'd be seen, Sam took Lindy into his arms and kissed her deeply. Then they said their goodbyes and Lindy returned to her mother.

"See, that wasn't so bad, was it?" her mother said, as they went back to the car.

"I could get used to it," Lindy said. And she meant it, too, just not in the way her mother hoped.

The internet was already working when Lindy got back to her room. She hadn't checked her social media sites in over a month, and she had hundreds of notifications. But the first thing she checked was her messages from Ronnie.

Lindy winced when she saw her last message. "I promise we'll get through this. I love you." She'd forgotten about that. She'd sent it right after the internet went out, so Ronnie wouldn't have received it until today. In retrospect, she shouldn't have said it. They'd only made out a couple of times, after all. Way too soon for the L word.

Apparently Ronnie agreed. "I'm sorry I can't do this," her message read. "I was just having fun. Maybe it's a good thing they sent me away. Sorry." Her message had just come across a few minutes earlier.

Lindy's fingers sped furiously over the keyboard. "I shouldn't have said it, I'm sorry. Please still be my friend." She hit Enter, but the message wouldn't send. Instead, she got a pop-up that said "You have been blocked from communicating with this user."

Her heart sank. The more she thought about it, the more she realized it hadn't actually been love, but rather the excitement of discovering a fellow lesbian-in-hiding. She'd have felt the same way about any girl who shared her interests. But that didn't lessen the blow. She'd lost a friend.

She wasn't sure how long she stared at her screen, rereading Ronnie's last message. But eventually she received a chat request. It was Sam.

"I had a great time today," he wrote.

"Me too!" Lindy replied. "I can't wait to do it again. Want to see a movie next weekend?"

"Sounds great," Sam wrote. "Can I ask you something about that kiss?"

"Wait," Lindy typed. They couldn't talk here. She'd

already given her mother a list of her passwords. For all Lindy knew, her mother might be logged in right now, monitoring this conversation on her tablet. Whatever Sam was wanting to ask, the question itself would probably reveal the kiss had been fake. They needed to take this conversation to a different chat program. Lindy would need to set up a new account, one her mother didn't know about.

"Take your time," Sam wrote.

"You're a really good kisser," Lindy typed. "I was just a little embarrassed that my mom was watching." Was that too subtle? She cringed in anticipation of Sam's reply.

"Say no more," Sam replied. "Next time we'll look for someplace with more privacy."

Lindy exhaled with relief. She wasn't sure if he'd gotten the message, but he did change the subject. They talked about their favorite movies, and after a while, Lindy forgot about her problems. It didn't matter that she'd lost her best friend, or that she no longer had any privacy. Sam was fun to talk to. He had a great sense of humor, and while he struggled to talk in person, he was really in his element with text chat. Some of his clever comebacks made Lindy laugh out loud.

I wish you were a girl, Lindy thought. For a moment, she even considered typing it. But then she remembered her mom might be watching. Suddenly nervous, she scrolled back over the chat history to make sure she hadn't typed anything incriminating. *This is no way to live*, she thought angrily.

The following weekend they went to see an action movie. Lindy's mom once again chaperoned, but she sat three rows behind them. During the movie, Lindy handed Sam a folded piece of paper. She whispered in his ear, asking him not to look at it until he got home. At the end of the date, they kissed again, just for show.

Once Lindy got home, she opened up her laptop. She

knew her mom wasn't a very technical person, so she probably didn't have to worry about any keylogger or screen sharing software. Nevertheless, she took a few precautions to make sure she wasn't being monitored. Once she felt reasonably safe, she logged into her secret chat account.

Sam had already set up an account, and Lindy friended him. "Good movie today," she typed.

"Loved it," Sam replied. "So can we talk? Really talk?"

"I think so. What was it you wanted to ask?"

"Why are we tricking your mom?"

Lindy thought a moment before typing. She was worried he wouldn't want to be her friend if they weren't dating. But were they really friends if they weren't honest with each other? "She caught me kissing a girl."

"Wow," Sam replied, punctuating the sentence with a wide-eyed emoji.

"Sorry if I led you on," Lindy typed.

"No worries. I like hanging out with you. You're fun. But as long as we're being honest…"

A few seconds passed. "Well?" Lindy typed.

"You're sure this is private?"

"I've done everything I can," Lindy replied. "I don't think mom will find out about this account. She thinks she knows more about computers than she really does."

"Okay, here goes," Sam typed. "Don't hate me…"

"Just rip off the bandage," Lindy wrote. "I won't judge."

"On these private chats, can you start calling me Samantha?"

Whoa, Lindy thought. She was surprised, but not really surprised. She thought she'd picked up a feminine vibe earlier, but she'd ignored it. Now she analyzed every interaction they'd had together, looking for clues she'd missed.

"Still there?" Samantha asked.

"Sorry, yes. Samantha it is. Do your parents know?"

"Not yet. But I plan on telling them soon."

"How do you think they'll take it?" Lindy typed.

"They're usually pretty open-minded, but I don't know."

"Good luck, Samantha," Lindy typed.

"I'm not seeing a lot of activity in your chat history," Lindy's mom said.

"I, uh, deleted the chat history when we were done talking," Lindy said. She knew her mother wouldn't like that explanation, but it was better than the truth.

Her mother glared at her. "You're not allowed any privacy right now," she said. "I can't be a good mother if I can't keep my eyes on you."

"Sorry. We were talking about, uh, sex stuff," Lindy lied. She tried to look embarrassed.

To Lindy's horror, her mother actually looked pleased. "Oh. Are you two thinking of taking things to the next level?"

"Mom!" Lindy exclaimed. "I can't talk about that with you!"

"Nonsense. You can talk to me about anything," her mother replied. "I won't judge."

Bullshit, Lindy thought. "Besides, you keep me locked up all the time. When would I even—"

"I've been thinking about that," her mother said. "You seem to be back on the right path. I was thinking about loosening the reigns a little."

"Really?" Lindy asked.

"I think you've earned it," her mother said. "I'm still watching you, though. I still want full access to your social media accounts and chats. But I'll stop locking your door, and you can even drive yourself to school again. Just be home by dinner. And no female friends."

That last demand was about to get more difficult.

"So what's the range on this thing?" Samantha asked,

watching the drone grow smaller in the distance. She was still presenting as a boy, but whenever the adults were out of earshot, she was Samantha. The two of them stood in Lindy's backyard, out by the airstrip.

"About half a mile," Lindy answered. "But that's nothing. I've got one upstairs with a range of seven miles." It was her eighteenth birthday, and she couldn't think of a better way to spend it than flying drones with a friend. Of course, that night she'd have cake with her parents, but she wasn't looking forward to that at all.

"That's awesome," Samantha said. "When you're sick, you could send it to school to pick up your homework."

"Or I could just download my homework from the school's website," Lindy said.

"Yeah, but this is cooler," Samantha said. She was getting a lot better at controlling it, and she made it take a weaving path back to them.

Lindy suddenly felt like she was being watched. She turned and looked up at the tower. There was too much glare to see through the glass, but she thought she saw movement in her room. She sighed. "I think mom's tossing my room again."

"Is there anything for her to find?" Samantha asked. The drone was only about fifty feet away now.

"Not really," Lindy said. "I even planted a couple of things that'll make her happy. Don't ask. But it still feels gross to have her pawing through my stuff."

"Sucks," Samantha said. "What did you – Whoa!" The drone took a nosedive, and crashed to the ground about ten feet away. Plastic pieces flew off in all directions.

They both ran toward the crash site, and Lindy knelt next to the drone. "I'm so sorry," Samantha said.

"Don't sweat it," Lindy replied. "This is totally fixable. Bring me the bag." Lindy picked up drone pieces while Samantha retrieved the drone's carrying case. There was a little toolkit inside, and Lindy pulled out a tiny screwdriver.

"Six minutes," she said. "Time me."

"You really know what you're doing," Samantha said, watching her work. "You could fix drones for a living. Have you picked a college yet?"

"That's up in the air right now," Lindy said. "I want to go as far away as possible, out from under mom's thumb. But she's afraid if she can't watch me, that I'll start dating girls. And for once, she's right."

"Well, you're way too smart for the schools in this town," Samantha said. "I'd hate to see you waste your life here. You know, my uncle works in admissions at an engineering school upstate. Maybe we could—"

"Unless it's within a ten-mile radius, I doubt mom'd let me," Lindy said. Then she set the drone on the ground, and took a few steps back. "Try it now."

Samantha switched on the controls, and soon the drone was airborne once again. "You're a genius," she said. "By the way, I've set a date. I'm coming out to my parents on Friday night."

Lindy leaned forward and kissed her. This time, it wasn't for show.

Saturday morning, Lindy woke up and sat up in bed. She was about to head towards the bathroom when she saw movement out of the corner of her eye. Her mother was sitting at the card table, watching her.

"What's wrong?" Lindy asked.

"You've been lying to me again," her mother said.

Lindy scrunched her face. Of course, she had been lying, but she couldn't imagine which lie her mother had caught. She decided to play innocent. "What do you mean?"

"Have you checked your social media today?" It was a dumb question, since she'd just seen Lindy wake up. But it was more of an accusation than a question, anyway. She held up her phone and showed it to her daughter.

Lindy gasped. Samantha had come out online, telling the

world her true name. Her new profile picture had her wearing a wig, makeup, and a dress. She looked beautiful. The comments were overwhelmingly supportive, including a couple from Samantha's parents. *Good for her,* Lindy thought.

"You knew about this, didn't you?" her mom asked.

Lindy nodded. It was pointless to lie.

"Obviously you can't see him again," her mother said.

"Mom—" Lindy started.

"I swear everyone in this state has gone crazy," her mom said. "Kids thinking they know more about themselves than their parents. Your schools are like indoctrination factories. They're supposed to teach you about heroes like Columbus and Edison. But instead they're encouraging you to change your biology or to marry your cat."

"Mom, that's not—"

"Well, you can kiss college goodbye. You're staying here until you're married. To a man. A real man. I'll find you someone. Someone who isn't crazy."

"Mom, you can't just—"

Her mother stood up. "I've taken away your wi-fi privileges. The world is a bad influence on you. From now on, it's school and home. Maybe not even school, if I can arrange it." She headed out the door, and started to slam it closed.

"No!" Lindy shouted, and grabbed the handle. They both pulled for a moment, until Lindy won out.

Her mother stood in the doorway, her eyes full of rage. She stepped forward and slapped Lindy's face. "Don't you dare defy me ever again!" she roared at her daughter.

Lindy was so shocked, she just stood there as her mother stepped back out of the room, slammed the door, and latched the outer lock.

"And don't think Sam's ever going to want to talk to you again!" her mother shouted from the other side of the door.

What did she mean by that? Lindy wondered, as she heard

her mother's steps descend the metal staircase. Then she had a horrible thought. She ran to her laptop and flipped it open.

Of course it wouldn't connect to the wi-fi, but she was still able to read her sent messages. Apparently she'd sent one to Samantha early this morning. Or rather, her mother had, posing as Lindy.

The message read: "Sam, I'm through with you. I never want to see your face again. How could I ever want to be with someone so mentally deranged? Boys can't be girls. Don't try to contact me again. P.S. – You make an ugly girl."

Lindy was stunned. *She'll never believe that was from me*, she thought. But she couldn't take that chance. Losing another friend was bad enough, but the breakup message was so cruel. If Samantha believed it, she'd be crushed. *I have to talk to her*, Lindy thought.

But how? She couldn't connect to wi-fi to send a message. She couldn't open her door. Her windows didn't open enough to climb out, and she'd kill herself getting down even if she did. Her cell phone could only call her parents. Samantha only lived six miles away, but it might as well have been six hundred.

She looked at her shelves. So many parts, so many tools. Maybe she could "engineer" her way out of the room somehow. Or maybe...

And then she got an idea.

Samantha sat on her bed, still in a daze. Showing the world who she really was had been one of the most euphoric things she'd ever done. For the most part, people had been supportive. A few of her classmates had made fun of her, but those guys made fun of everyone. The opinions of morons meant nothing to her.

Lindy's opinion, on the other hand, meant everything. Reading her message had felt like getting punched in the gut. It didn't even sound like something Lindy would say. *Maybe she was just trying to please her mom,* Samantha thought. It wouldn't be the first time. A few weeks earlier, Lindy's mom had complained that she couldn't read Lindy's chat history. Ever since then, they'd used one chat for safe topics like movies, and the private chat for real talk. Occasionally they'd flirt a little in the regular chat, just so Lindy's mom wouldn't complain again. Could this have been another attempt to throw off her mother's scent?

But if so, why wasn't Lindy answering the private chat? She hadn't answered any of Samantha's messages since sending the breakup note. Apparently Lindy was just done with her. Samantha wasn't the most social person in the world. It took her a while to warm up to people. But she and Lindy had just clicked, and the thought of losing her was too much to bear.

There was a commotion outside, like a lawnmower trying to cut through a steel pipe. Samantha stood up and ran to her window. A drone was caught in the tree in her backyard. Samantha ran outside and climbed up the tree. She switched off the drone, disentangled it from the branches, and took it back to her room. *This has to be from Lindy,* she thought. *But why?* She turned the drone over a few times, looking for clues. She opened the battery compartment, removed the memory card, and inserted it into her computer.

The root directory included some system files and a folder for pictures. It also included a text file named "SAMANTHA README." It read: "Samantha, I hope this drone makes it to you. I programmed the GPS with your address, but anything could happen between here and there. I'm so sorry. That hurtful message wasn't from me. My mother wrote it, right before she took away my internet. Please, I need your help. I'm a prisoner in my own home. My parents go to bed around ten. Please show up at midnight. Just stand beneath my south window, I'll do the rest. But if you can't make it, just know this: You are valid, and I love you. With or without me, please live a great life, as the person you were meant to be."

At ten-til-midnight, Lindy sat by an open window, her suitcase by her side. It was too dark to see much below. She wanted to yell something out the window, but she was also afraid to make any noise. She wondered if Samantha was already here, or if she was coming at all. Did she even get the drone? Would she be able to sneak out of her house? Would she even care enough to come? Lindy had used the L word again in that message, and now she hoped it wasn't a mistake.

Five minutes before midnight, she heard an owl. Actually, it sounded almost nothing like an owl, but rather a teenager's voice shouting "Who! Who!" Lindy laughed. She dangled her keys out the window, letting them jingle for a few seconds, and dropped them to the ground. A few minutes later she heard footsteps coming up the metal stairs. She heard the outer latch slide aside, and the door opened.

Lindy and Samantha flew into each other's arms, hugging so tight they could barely breathe. "I love you too," Samantha said. Lindy grabbed her suitcase, and the two ran down the stairs, out the door, and into the night.

Samantha's mother was a lawyer, and she had no trouble drawing up the paperwork to keep Lindy out of her parents' hands. Lindy applied for several college grants, and ended up with multiple options for nearly-free tuition. She stayed with Samantha's family until graduation, then she and Samantha went off to college together.

Lindy and Samantha never actually became a couple, and by the time they graduated college, each had found the person they would eventually marry. But their friendship remained strong, and the two couples became like family.

And when Lindy finally had children of her own, she made sure to listen to them, to respect them, and to let them explore their own identities.

Mother's Day

Thump.

It was just a single thump, a random sound that could have been anything. Maybe a picture fell off the wall. Maybe the fridge did some "cooling cycle" thing. Maybe a tree branch landed on the roof.

Or maybe someone was trying to break in. Jo lay quietly in bed, her dream fading. She listened intently for further noises, but the night was silent. She moved her sleep mask up to her forehead so she could look at her alarm clock. It was nearly three in the morning. She had to be up in another three hours.

She closed her eyes again, and kept listening for more noises. The original thump had shifted her heart into overdrive, and she was just now starting to calm down again. She wondered if she'd be able to fall back asleep, but she also knew that stressing about it was a sure-fire way to keep from doing it. She tried not to think about falling asleep, but that just made the thoughts more pervasive. So she tried not thinking about not thinking about sleep, which got her thinking about wordplay, which reminded her of her writer friend back in college, and whatever happened to her anyway?

This string of thoughts eventually led to her other college friends, and that boyfriend who dropped out to become a race car driver, and cars in general, and then she remembered that her own car was overdue for an oil change, and she really needed to write that on the calendar, and just like that she was wide awake again. She took another look at the clock. Fifteen minutes had passed. She was about to close her eyes again when she felt the call of nature.

Her alarm clock was annoyingly bright even on the dim setting, so she had no problem navigating the bedroom. Once she got into the hallway, however, it was pitch black. She felt her way along the wall until she reached the bathroom, and turned on the light. She was about to enter her bathroom when she heard another sound from downstairs. It was a light whimpering, like that of an injured animal.

The bathroom door was across from the stairs, and a small amount of light made it down the stairwell. It revealed something odd at the bottom of the stairs, something still half-hidden in the darkness, something Jo couldn't quite make out but it definitely hadn't been there when she'd gone to bed. She took a step towards the stairwell, squinting for a better look. It looked like a bundle of laundry, but all black and gray.

Then her eyes focused. The gray became pallid skin, and the black became hair. Some... *thing* was sitting on the bottom step of her stairwell, everything but its back obscured by the shadow of the banister. She let out a small gasp, and the visitor's head turned to look at her. A yellow eye peeked out from behind its long, greasy bangs.

Suddenly it moved, turning around as it rose. Jo backed into the bathroom. The thing had started moving with unnerving speed. It was halfway up the stairs by the time she'd taken three steps backward. It climbed the stairs on all fours, with unnaturally long arms and legs, way out of proportion to the rest of its body.

Jo slammed the door and locked it, then braced her back against the door. Barely a second passed before something pounded against the door, threatening to knock it down. Then the pounding stopped, replaced by a scraping sound, moving its way down the door. Jo looked down to see four gray fingers slide underneath the door, knuckles down, fingertips curling up toward her. Each finger was as long as Jo's entire hand, and tipped with cracked, yellow fingernails.

Jo shrieked as she felt something touch her heel. The other set of fingers brushed against the side of her foot. Jo stomped on the fingers, which elicited a low howl from the other side of the door. She rushed to the bathroom sink and grabbed the first object she saw, a large brush. Then she jumped into the shower and closed the clear, frosted door.

The pounding came again, and then the door burst open. Jo couldn't make out a lot of details through the frosted glass. The not-quite-human form lurched forward, its unusual proportions distorted even further by the translucent door. The blurred form reached towards the shower, those gray fingers folding over the top of the glass.

Jo cowered in the corner, sitting on the floor of the shower, hugging her knees. She couldn't find her voice to scream, and instead made deep sobbing sounds. The thing found the edge of the door and slid it aside. Then the creature's head poked into the shower, supported by an unusually long and flexible neck. The head turned toward Jo, and it smiled. Its teeth were just as yellow and ragged as its nails.

"Muhrr…" it said.

Jo finally found it in her to scream, but she only had time to do it once.

"So what have you got for me?" Detective Hanover asked, as the officer handed her a manilla folder.

"White female, thirty-six, found dead in her shower," Officer Collins said.

Hanover sipped her coffee. "Killer must be a Hitchcock

fan," she said.

"I doubt this killer has the patience for movies," Collins said. "The victim was ripped to shreds. It looked like the work of a wild animal."

"Then why me? This should go to Animal Control or the Department of Wildlife."

"Her wounds are too ragged to be a knife, but they don't look like any animal claws on record. And it left these weird, elongated fingerprints. The coroner's calling it a cryptid."

"I see," Hanover said with a sigh. That explained why it was landing on her desk. The two biggest successes of her career had been occult-related. In both cases, the killers had tried to make the crime look supernatural, and some of the officers had even fallen for it. But Hanover had a knack for seeing through bullshit. She was starting to get a reputation as the department's resident party pooper, as she was always the first one to pop the balloon when a new urban legend began to spread. She supposed there were worse ways to make a name for yourself, but she didn't want to get shoehorned into always getting handed the paranormal-themed assignments.

But someone had to, and she seemed to be the best at it. "Let's go," she said, standing up.

Detective Hanover had never seen a crime scene like it. The front and back door were locked, and none of the first-floor windows were broken. In fact, nothing appeared out of the ordinary on the first floor at all, except for some odd patches of soot on the carpet. The house had no chimney, so Hanover wasn't sure where the soot might have come from.

Upstairs, the hallway bathroom was a nightmare. The victim hadn't just been torn apart, she'd been... *Weeded,* Hanover thought. It was the best word she could come up with. It was as if the victim had been a garden, and the attacker had plucked her organs out like weeds. The organs weren't missing, however; they had been placed back into the victim's chest cavity, though not necessarily where they belonged. The killer – be they man or animal – hadn't actually needed the organs. They hadn't eaten them or stolen them.

So, why? Hanover wondered. It was perfectly possible that the killer was simply insane, and there was no reason for their actions. But Hanover had dealt with insane killers before, and even they had motives, even if those motives were based on delusions. If a killer had a motive, you could predict their behavior. All she had to do was figure out why this killer did what they did.

She followed the blood trail from the bathroom to the bedroom, where it led to a broken window. The window had been smashed from the inside. The officers had found a bit more blood on the roof, but no further trail on the ground outside.

"We have an exit but no entry point," Hanover said, thinking out loud.

"She must have let the guy in," Collins said.

Hanover nodded. "I want to talk to everyone she knew, especially the men."

"There's still something else I need to show you," Collins said. "In the basement."

The house didn't have a full basement, it was more of a storage room for the water heater. Still, there were a few square feet left over, and Jo had apparently made use of it in the strangest way. A red circle was painted on the concrete floor, with rune-like symbols around the perimeter. The remnants of burned-out candles surrounded the circle at regular intervals.

"So, the victim was, what, into witchcraft?" Hanover asked.

"Beats me," Collins answered, scratching his head.

"Well, get me that list of friends and relatives," Hanover ordered. "Maybe they'll know what she was doing here."

* * *

For a New Age shop, Tori's Cauldron didn't seem too mystical. Hanover wasn't sure what she'd expected, but this just looked like your average mom-and-pop bookstore, except the occult section took up more space. Detective Hanover and the shop's owner, Tori Lewis, sat in the shop's office. Tori was in her early thirties, with short, black hair. Again subverting Hanover's expectations, Tori did not wear cultist robes or a tattered black dress, but rather a plain white T-shirt and overalls.

"I'm sorry for your loss, Ms. Lewis," Hanover said.

"Please call me Tori," the shopkeeper answered, wiping her nose with a tissue.

"And you can call me Hope," Hanover said. "Can you tell me what was going on in your friend's basement?" She handed her a photo of the painted circle.

Tori examined the photo and nodded. "Jo was my best friend, but she didn't always make the best decisions." She blew her nose before continuing. "She wanted a baby. It's all she ever wanted. But she didn't want a relationship, and she couldn't afford any of the alternatives."

"You're saying she was trying to get pregnant... using magic?" Hanover asked.

"You're not very spiritual, are you?" Tori asked.

"Not really," Hanover answered. "But even back when I was, I only believed in one divine birth. Surely Jo didn't believe she could get pregnant through a spell."

"I don't think she knew what to expect. Maybe pregnancy, but maybe she just thought a baby would get left on her doorstep." Tori handed the photo back, and stared hard into Hanover's eyes. "But she wished for a child, and that's what clawed its way into our world... a child. Just not the species she was hoping for."

I can't believe this is the best lead I have, Hanover thought, frowning. But the wounds she'd examined earlier... it did seem like they could have been the result of curiosity. Like a child taking apart a toy truck, and being unable to put it back together. She looked at the picture again, then back at Tori.

The sincerity in Tori's eyes gave Hanover pause. She found the woman's words compelling, even though she was talking nonsense. Hanover didn't believe what Tori was saying, but she believed that Tori believed it. This wasn't some charlatan trying to sell her some snake oil. This was just a woman with a different worldview, who sincerely wanted to help.

"Detective Han… Hope," Tori said. "I know you don't believe any of this. And that's okay. You don't have to. But supernatural monster or demented killer, it has to be stopped. I have an idea, but I'll need your help."

Hope wasn't sure how Tori had talked her into this. She wasn't even on duty, and this was against every protocol, and it might have even been illegal. The pair currently sported matching shovels, and were digging in a shallow cave. It was well after midnight, and their only light came from the headlights of Hope's car.

After just a few minutes of digging, Tori pulled a locket out of the ground. "One artifact down, only twelve to go!" she said.

"There's been another murder," Officer Collins said, handing Detective Hanover several documents and photos.

Hanover exhaled, took a sip of coffee, and looked at the photos. "Pull in everyone you can," she said. "Ask up and down the neighborhood. See if anyone caught this thing on their doorbell cameras."

"This… thing?" Collins asked. "Don't you mean, this murderer?"

"Of course," Hanover said. "But anyone capable of… *this* doesn't deserve to be called human." She pointed at one of the photos for emphasis, but she wasn't sure if she was trying to convince Collins or herself.

Hope had officially crossed the line between "legally gray area" and "if I get caught, my career is over." Fortunately the mausoleum had no security cameras, so her job was probably safe. She still wasn't convinced that there was any point to this, but if there was even the tiniest chance that this harmless grave robbing would save a life, it was worth it.

But was that the real reason? Hope watched Tori's exuberant face as she pulled the ring off of the dead woman's finger. Her eyes sparkled as she held the ring up to examine it with her flashlight. Tori had a way of making it almost… fun? Was it right to have fun when investigating a killer? But then, when wasn't Hope investigating a killer? She had to have fun sometime, or she'd crack.

At least Tori was no longer a suspect. The previous night's murder had occurred while Hope was with Tori, so she couldn't have been involved.

"You look like fewmets today," Collins said. It was a little game they had. There was a curse jar in the office, to which Hanover had contributed more than her share in the past. Now she and Collins tried to outdo each other, each trying to come up with the most creative and obscure synonyms for excrement. "Did you sleep at all last night?"

"Not really," Hanover answered, but didn't elaborate. She wasn't about to tell him what she'd been up to after her shifts. "Those lab tests come back yet?"

"Yeah, but they were inconclusive. They couldn't even tell if the hairs were human or animal. Chuck says they're going to mail the sample to the good lab."

Ugh, Hanover thought. That meant it would be another week before they got any results. How many more would die in the meantime? At least there hadn't been any new murders today. Yet.

* * *

"Not bad for a sixth date, eh?" Tori remarked, as they fled the museum. Hope was so preoccupied with running that she didn't even register the significance of the d-word.

They'd almost gotten out without setting off the alarm. Luckily the fingerbone on display was just a replica. The actual artifact was underground in the museum archives, or it had been until a few minutes ago. Ironically, it was easier to break into the archives than the actual museum, especially with Hope's connections. But they'd still managed to trip an alarm on the way out.

"Same time tomorrow?" Hope asked, as they got into her car.

"Do you have to go home so soon?" Tori asked. "I was hoping we could grab a cup of coffee."

Hope looked at the car's clock. It was half past midnight. "I suppose I could spare half an hour." She drove them to a place called "Drew's All-Nighter," a favorite spot for cops and college students. It was nearly empty, and they found a quiet booth.

"So what's tomorrow?" Hope asked, as she slid into her seat.

"Should be easy," Tori said. "There's this guy, lives on East Terrace. He's a collector. He has a jewel in his collection, that once belonged to a Pharoah. He's out of town for the week, and has weak security."

"How do you know this?" Hope asked.

Tori frowned. "You wouldn't believe me."

Hope put her hand on her face. "Tell me you're not basing this on crystal balls and psychic flashes."

"Not... exactly," Tori said. "I used a Ouija board." She took a long sip of her coffee, waiting for Hope's reaction.

Hope groaned. "I'm trying to solve a murder here, and you're having imaginary conversations with dead people. How am I supposed to take any of this seriously?"

"It hasn't been wrong yet," Tori said.

"Seriously?" Hope asked.

"That's how I knew the finger would be in the museum archives."

"By talking to ghosts," Hope said. Her tone was neutral. She didn't believe it, but she wanted to hear her friend out.

"I don't think it's a ghost," Tori said. "It calls itself Mur. I think it's from... somewhere else."

"Why not just ask Mur where the killer is?" Hope turned her head as a police car drove by outside. She realized it was probably headed to the museum.

"It's not omniscient, or precognizant," Tori said. "It just has a perspective we don't."

"Not that I believe in Ouija boards," Hope said, "but have you considered that this 'Mur' might be using you? Maybe it wants you to collect these artifacts for some other reason."

"I have," Tori said. "But I've also researched the spell in question. They're the right ingredients for what we want to do. Even if it wants it for the wrong reasons, it's the right spell."

Hope sighed. "I don't even know what my life is anymore," she said. In one week she'd gone from skeptic cop to paranormal thief. Except it hadn't really taken a week. Somehow, she'd been on board from the very first day. She still wasn't sure how Tori had talked her into all this. She kept telling herself it was because lives were at stake, and it was the only lead they had... but no, even on her most desperate day Hope wouldn't have jumped right into helping a witch steal spell ingredients.

Then she looked into Tori's eyes and she remembered. There was something about those eyes, something that made Hope want to do whatever the woman asked. Did Tori feel the same way?

"Don't worry," Tori said, smiling softly. "Your life will go back to normal as soon as we finish the spell."

Hope nodded, but she wondered if she even wanted to resume her normal life. Always surrounded by death, going from one crime scene to the next, never having time for friends… or lovers. Tori seemed to have made a nice life for herself, running her little shop. It seemed so idyllic. She pictured herself stocking the shelves, balancing the books, repairing worn-out fixtures…

"What?" Tori asked.

Hope realized she had zoned out, staring into Tori's eyes. "Nothing," she finally said. "Just, it's time I got some sleep." They stood up, paid for their orders, and walked out the door. As Hope pulled up to Tori's place to let her out, they shared a brief kiss. It felt so natural, that Hope was halfway home before she suddenly realized it had been their first kiss.

While she only got about five hours of sleep, Hanover was in a good mood the next day. She kept finding herself whistling, something she hadn't done since she was in high school. She made sure to tone it down once she got to the station, but Collins still noticed.

"Sounds like somebody got some last night," Collins said. "Who is she?"

"Give me a break," Hanover said, her face suddenly hot.

"Oh my god, I'm right, aren't I. I've never seen you blush like that."

"Collins, I swear," Hanover said.

But before Collins could say anything more, Officer Phillips burst into the office. "There's been two more murders," he said breathlessly.

The crime scene was similar to the others, only there were two victims this time. A retired married couple, disassembled and reassembled like toy building blocks, some parts reattached to the wrong body. The house was three streets over from the original murder. So far all the deaths had been within a five-mile radius.

They collected plenty of evidence but no new insights.

Hanover brooded all the way back to the station. They needed to step things up. Not the police force, they were already doing all they could. It was crazy, but Hope was making more headway with the occult angle than with police procedure.

But they had fewer than half the artifacts, and people were dying. They couldn't keep going at this pace, collecting one artifact each night. Hanover knew what she had to do.

"Denied," Chief Parvelli said.

"What?" Hanover asked. "I have eight weeks of vacation saved up."

"Not while you're in the middle of such a big case," Parvelli said.

"Give it to Detective Latham," Hanover suggested. "He's —"

"He's already overworked," the chief said. "Besides, he's not —"

"My mother died," Hanover said.

"Three years ago, I remember," Chief Parvelli said. "I went with you to her funeral."

"I've been an exemplary employee," Hanover said. "I've earned —"

"Yes, you have," Parvelli said. "You're the best we have right now. Which is why I'm sure you'll catch this creep within the week, and then you can take all the time off you want."

Hanover glared, red-faced. "Sir, if you would just —"

"You have my decision, Detective."

Hanover took a few steps towards the door. Then she stopped. *Lives are at stake*, she reminded herself. She balled up her fist and turned back to her superior.

"Who's in there with Parvelli?" Collins asked. The shouting match from inside the office was audible throughout the department.

"Hanover," Officer Mullins replied. "I don't know what it's about, though."

The yelling continued for several minutes, until there was a thump sound that made several officers move towards the door. Then Parvelli started yelling again. The only word they could make out was "suspended."

The door opened, and Hanover stepped out. She looked angry, and wouldn't look anyone in the eye. Parvelli watched her from his office doorway, a bruise forming on his left cheek.

Hanover went to her desk and took out a few personal items. Collins tried to approach her but she waved him off. She left without saying a word. She got into her car, started the ignition, and looked at herself in the rearview mirror.

And she smiled.

The circle was drawn, with the thirteen artifacts placed at regular intervals around the perimeter. Hope placed a tuft of that mysterious hair into the center of the circle, then stepped back out. Tori began reading Latin phrases from a book. When she finished, the floor inside the circle shimmered, and Hope's jaw dropped open. She wasn't sure at what point she'd started believing in this stuff, but her mind had opened a lot in the past couple of weeks. Still, this was the first undeniably paranormal event she'd witnessed.

"Wow," Hope said.

"Creature from beyond our realm," Tori said, "Come to us, return to your home." The round patch of floor now rippled like water, and glowed.

Hope looked around her basement. "Where is it? Is it just supposed to appear, or..."

"I don't know," Tori said. "Believe it or not, this is the first time I've done this."

Suddenly a large gray hand thrust out of the rippling portal. It was soon joined by another. The hands gripped the edges of the portal and pulled.

"Something's coming out," Hope said, drawing her gun. "Nothing should be coming out, we're supposed to be sending stuff in!"

"Just stay away from it," Tori said. "Don't shoot unless it threatens us."

The two women backed as far away from the circle as they could. The creature pulled itself out and stood in the basement, one foot on each side of the circle. It was huge – way too big to be the thing that killed those victims. This creature couldn't have fit in Jo's bathroom. It crouched now, trying to find a tenable position. Hope's basement had a relatively high ceiling, but this creature had to stay low or bump its head. With its shoulders nearly touching the ceiling, its head stayed at about chest height, suspended by a long, snakelike neck. Its long black hair hung over most of its wrinkled, crone-like face.

"Baab," it shouted, looking around the room. Its round, yellowed eyes centered on Tori. "BAAB!" it shouted again, reaching for her. Hope stepped in front of Tori, her weapon aimed at the monster.

"Don't fire," Tori hissed in Hope's ear. "You'll just make it mad!"

There was a crash from upstairs. The door to the basement burst open. Another gray creature slinked down the steps on giant hands and feet. It ignored the women and looked straight at the larger creature. "Murrh!" it growled happily.

"It looks just like its mother," Tori said, backing up against the wall as it passed.

"Baab!" the larger creature shouted. The younger monster leaped into its mother's arms, and they hugged. The mother gave Tori one last look that might have meant thank you, then the pair of creatures disappeared into the portal. Tori quickly ended the spell before anything else came through.

Hope and Tori hugged for several minutes, then cleaned

up all the artifacts.

Six months later, Officer Collins strolled into Tori's Cauldron. "Hey, Hanover," he said, with a smile and a wave.

From behind the counter, Hope stood up and greeted her former partner. "Did you bring it?" she asked, casting a sideways glance at the back room.

"Freshly resized," Collins whispered, tossing a small box into Hope's outstretched hand.

She snapped open the box, took a long look at the beautiful engagement ring, and shoved it into her pocket.

"So, tonight's the big night?" Collins asked.

"The big night for what?" Tori asked, walking out of the back room. "Hi, Collins."

"I was just telling him about our dinner plans," Hope said. "Best steak in town, I can't wait."

"Ah," Tori said. "And here I thought you were talking about that engagement ring."

"Uh, ring?" Collins asked. "She didn't say anything about a ring."

"Really," Tori said, smiling. "Three diamonds, ruby chip in the center? Mur says it's huge."

"Who's Mur?" Collins asked, but Hope just stood there with her mouth open. Had she still been talking to that creature? Collins looked back and forth between them for a moment, wondering what was going on.

Then Tori burst out laughing. "The security camera, you dope. It's right behind the register. I was watching the monitor in the back room."

Hope laughed with relief, and gave Tori a hug. Collins still wasn't sure what "Mur" meant, but he laughed along with them. With the surprise now blown, Hope dropped down to one knee right there. Maybe they weren't at a fancy restaurant, but it didn't matter. Being with Tori made anywhere special, and Hope never wanted to leave her side again.

Fairy Dust

The wind flowed across the plain, gently tickling the grass and barely disrupting the many sets of butterfly wings as they flitted from flower to flower. On first inspection, a casual observer might simply have said "Wow, the bugs sure grow big around here," before continuing to enjoy the breeze. But a closer look would have revealed much more fascinating creatures: tiny winged people, happily singing while tending the garden.

These were the fairies, the magical fey folk, carefree lovers of life, simple-minded protectors of nature. These minute hovering gardeners went about their work with extraordinary zeal, and our hypothetical observer would have wondered if this was work or recreation. There were thirty-one of them today, following their usual routine, each focused on their specific job. An insect-like grig tilled the soil with the help of a large stag beetle. He was followed by a wingless brownie, who dug small holes in the loose dirt. A highly-energetic pixie planted palm-sized flower seeds, carefully burying one at a time. A nixie then walked by sprinkling water over the dirt. Finally, a tiny sprite sprinkled fairy dust over the planted seeds, which insured quick growth. This chain of workers was mirrored throughout the garden, each group concentrating on a different species of flower. A single dryad supervisor walked among them, stepping carefully and monitoring the quality of their work.

They sang as they worked, a freeform, wordless tune that conveyed the joy in their hearts. For them, all was right with the world, and they were one with nature. The flowers that grew would be used for potions and nectar, and would eventually yield seeds so they could plant even more flowers. The fairies would always be able to rely on their crops, and they always gave back more than they took. Such was the pleasure they took in the cycle of nature, that they were never short of volunteers for the job. For as Delia the Fairy Queen was fond of saying, "Mini hands make light work."

THUMP!

The singing stopped. Thirty-one sets of ears perked up.

THUMP!

Thirty-one heads looked up from their flowers, searching for the source of the noise.

THUMP! THUMP! CRACK!

A tree fell over in the distance. The fairies turned in that direction just in time to see a great reptilian head burst through the treeline.

"It's a red!" shouted a pixie, and the gardeners scattered. A few fairies succumbed to fear and fled into the forest, but most went for their weapons. As the dragon pushed past the last few trees and entered the clearing, he was greeted by a swarm of tiny arrows. Most bounced harmlessly off his crimson scales, but a few managed to slip beneath them and pierce the monster's skin. These pinpricks were no more than a nuisance, however, and the dragon responded with a large belch of flames.

Any dragon was bad enough, but a fire-breathing red was particularly unwanted by this plant-loving group. The dryad supervisor now fled in terror, having been turned into a living torch by the monster's breath. She nearly reached the treeline before collapsing into a heap of kindling.

Two nixies tried to put her out, but it was a lost cause. "Charge!" yelled a fearless brownie, leading the remaining gardners-turned-warriors toward their enemy, while a few sprites and pixies chanted out protection charms.

The dragon was outnumbered, but it was much more powerful than the tiny army it faced. It was sure to be a short battle.

Some distance away, Queen Delia emerged from her bath. She was beauty and grace personified, born of pixie but sired by a human. Such pairings were rare, and physically impossible without growth potions or other magic. It was a union that seldom produced offspring, and such progeny were often well-gifted in magical ability. The Queen was much taller than most of her subjects, nearly half the size of a human, with a pair of translucent golden wings that glittered in the light.

As she crossed her chambers, two sprite attendants dried her skin with an oakleaf towel, and perfumed her perfect body with lilac essence. Then the sprites helped her into a robe of the finest golden silkleaf, which matched the color of her wings. A third attendant entered with a plate of assorted ripe berries, along with a cup of the finest mix of nectar and honeysuckle juice. The Queen took a small sip from the cup, and strode over to the balcony.

Fairies didn't hoard wealth any more than dragons planted gardens. But the Grand Oak Palace was exquisite nonetheless. Built atop the oldest, tallest tree in the forest, the wooden palace was formed from the living tree itself. The pinnacle of dryad construction, the palace hadn't been built so much as grown. The floor was composed of closely intertwined branches, which curved sharply upwards to form the walls. The branches were so well-knit that they even held in a layer of dirt, upon which more plants grew. The Queen's chambers more closely resembled a park than a bedroom, complete with stone paths and chirping birds.

From a distance, the palace was virtually invisible, though the tree did stand out simply by virtue of being so tall. From the balconies, the Queen could see her entire kingdom. The treehouses of Fairy Haven, the peaceful Nixie Lake, Grig Burrows, the beautiful Fairy Gardens... The Queen stopped. There was a thin black line rising from the gardens. She chanted a spell, causing her eyes to glow brightly. Now she could see the gardens more closely, and what she saw terrified her. Fire and smoke, and the occasional flash of red scales. The Queen turned quickly, calling to her attendant. "Kora... Ah!" She had turned to find herself staring directly into Kora's huge eyes, startling her until she realized that the attendant was actually hovering on the other side of the room, enlarged only by the Queen's vision spell. It would have been funny if not for the emergency.

"Kora, send a squad to the garden. We have a Code Red."

"Red? Right away, Mum." The sprite flitted out the door. The Queen didn't watch her go, instead turning back to the view from the balcony. Kora knew the drill. The squad would be dressed in fireproof gear, carry cold-enchanted weapons, and the squad's wizards would have freezing spells ready to cast. Additionally, a nixie cleanup crew would be on standby to put out the garden. And when it was over, the Magic Council would investigate the magical barrier which - usually - prevented dragons from crossing into the Fairy Kingdom.

The fairies had dealt with this before; they knew what to do.

Another burst of smoke and fire blossomed from the dragon's mouth. A tiny sprite managed to survive the flames, having protected herself with an incantation. Her success was short-lived, however, as a huge clawed foot came down on top of her. She was killed instantly, leaving nothing but a cloud of sparkling fairy dust, which swirled and danced away as it mixed with the smoke from the blazing garden.

"Fall back! Fall back!" yelled the final surviving pixie, retreating to the cover of the forest. One of her legs was badly burned, and her leafy skirt was on fire, but she ignored both in favor of firing more arrows at the great lizard. Below her line of fire, she could see a pair of sprites fleeing in her direction, and a nixie trying to drag a mortally wounded grig out of harm's way. The brownies were long gone, their fearlessness leading to their early deaths in the battle. The pixie nocked another arrow, gritting her teeth in anger. She knew it was a losing battle, but she intended to go down fighting.

Suddenly it got very cold. A huge gust of wind blew through the garden, and the sky darkened. Fluffy snowflakes fell lazily to the earth, mixed with light freezing rain. The rain quickly grew in severity, until large chunks of ice were falling from the sky. There was a loud shout of "Charge!" and twenty fairy soldiers entered the fray. The frontline consisted of ten brownie swordmasters, carrying shields enchanted against fire. Behind them was a line of eight pixie archers, firing powerful enchanted arrows at the dragon's most vital areas. At the back of the squad stood two pixie wizards, responsible for the sudden change in weather. All the soldiers were wearing the exquisite golden uniforms of the Queen's elite guard, with bright red shoulder pads to indicate that the uniforms were enchanted against fire.

The dragon could not last long against such a group. Its most powerful weapon was effectively useless against the soldiers, and so the dragon had to rely on tooth and claw. He was still the strongest of the combatants, and could easily tear a fairy to shreds. But his opponents were simply too small and quick for him. They deftly dodged his claws, ducked his attempts to bite them, and leaped over the sweeps of his tail. And for every swipe he missed, his own hide was punctured by dozens of tiny arrows, his belly pierced by tiny blades, and his head bashed by flying icicles.

When a well-aimed arrow caught him in the eye, he knew he'd had enough. He turned and fled back out of the grove, taking the same path of fallen trees he'd forged on his way in. But the soldiers weren't about to just let him get away. They followed the beast through the trees, easily keeping up with the tiring monster. They reached another clearing, and the dragon finally collapsed. The fairies formed a large circle around the helpless beast, and quickly executed him.

Never ones to waste good spellcasting components, the two wizards started passing out vials, which the soldiers began filling with dragon blood. Once all the blood had been drained, the wizards cast a spell to dissolve the body. One of the archers fired a flare arrow into the sky, which signaled the nixie cleanup crew that it was time to head for the garden. Wounds were bandaged, arrows were retrieved, and finally the soldiers lined up to head back to the Garden.

Suddenly, they found themselves surrounded. All around the clearing, dragons faded into existence. Two more reds, a green, a yellow, a blue, and two purples - the last two responsible for the powerful invisibility spell which had allowed for their dramatic entrance. Before the soldiers even had time to be surprised, the dragons opened their mouths and let loose blasts of deadly breath.

The Queen watched it all through a small scrying orb. Her twenty best soldiers... no, not just soldiers, these were also her friends. Two of them had even been her blanket companions in the past. But she had no time for tears. "Kora!" she called. Before Kora could even respond, the Queen commanded, "Code Rainbow."

The first dragon had been a ruse. She'd thought it was a random rogue, who'd blundered through a weak spot in the barrier. But packs of dragons tended to stick with companions of like color. This had to be a coordinated attack, planned in advance by the Dragon War Council. This meant that the dragon sorcerers had discovered a counterspell for the barrier. Worse, it probably meant that more dragon packs had made it through. The Queen rushed back to her balcony.

And there it was. More columns of smoke drifted skyward, at key points throughout the kingdom. The invasion had begun.

On the Southern border of the Fairy Kingdom, there rested a small village called Proudpath. To the local farmers, the existence of fairies was a topic of frequent discussion. Living so close to the fairy regions meant that there had certainly been more sightings than in the average town. Just a few weeks prior, a pair of children had been lost in the woods, only to be guided back to safety by a kind sprite. And there were many more such "fairy tales." A mortally injured villager was healed by a tiny angel, strange lights scared a pack of wolves away from a young girl, and even the local shoemaker had received mysterious help when he became too ill to keep up with his business. But the debate was still there - were these truly fairies, or help from the gods themselves?

In truth, the villagers enjoyed the mystery. It was fun watching the fireflies off in the woods at night, and wondering if they were truly insects or actually fairies. It made for great campfire talk, and gave them material for bedtime stories.

Today there was to be no mystery. As the dragons advanced through the village, indiscriminately smashing houses with no more remorse than they had for the trees, the fairies fought back in full view of the frightened villagers. The fey folk were all the more careful with innocent humans about. The dragons showed no such consideration, and that gave them a tremendous advantage. The fairies were beaten back, wounded, and chased into the forest by their enemies. The surviving humans watched helplessly as the final dragon marched out of Proudpath, pursuing the fey into the woods. On a better day, the villagers might have taken up arms against the dragons, but at this moment they were in no shape for battle.

"Take me to Torrentia," the Fairy Queen ordered. She was quickly escorted from the palace, through the surrounding grounds, and to the caves. A guard saluted as she strode past, and two more guards opened the door to the prison for her. On one side of the giant cell, two sleeping dragons snored loudly. In the opposite corner, a woman sat on the floor, examining her fingernails. The Queen entered the cell, and the inmate rose to meet her.

"My Queen," Torrentia said, doing a mock curtsy. In her current human form, Torrentia was much taller than the Fairy Queen. She was beautiful, but it was a harsher kind of beauty, much different from the Queen's delicate features. She had angular cheekbones, dark eyes, long silver hair, and grayish skin so pale it was almost translucent. She wore a flowing dress that appeared to be made of silver scales. Torrentia faced the Queen with a sarcastic half-smile, showing no fear of her captor.

"Torrentia Wyvernica Demonicus," the Queen acknowledged, not the least bit intimidated by the woman.

"Queen Rainshower Sunbow Moonbeam," the woman replied.

"That was three queens ago," Queen Delia answered.

"My apologies. Shows how long I've been locked up here... and you fey folk do look so alike to me," Torrentia said wryly. "So... to what do I owe the—"

"I have not the time for pleasantries," the Queen interrupted. "As much as I hate to do this, I need your help."

"Go on," the woman said, but her smile told the whole story. She already knew of the attack.

"Drive them off," the Queen demanded.

"And my incentive?" Torrentia's tone was playful, and it was obvious she knew what the Queen would offer.

"Your freedom, of course," the Queen answered.

"And the full terms of this freedom?" The woman looked

down at her wrists, which were bound with glowing magical loops.

"You will order the dragons out of my kingdom. If they do not obey, you will use deadly force."

"Against my own kind? I think n—"

The Queen would not be interrupted. "Once the dragons are gone, you will immediately return to your den in the Northern Regions. You will stay in the Northern Regions, and never trouble my kingdom again."

"How do you expect to enforce that?"

"By your word," the Queen replied. "Your bracelets are bound by my magic. If you give me your word, and truly intend to honor that promise, then the bracelets will come undone. If you intend to deceive me, the binding spell will continue."

Torrentia looked thoughtful for several seconds. "Very well," she said finally. "You have my word. I will fix your little dragon problem, and return to my homeland for good." As soon as the words were out of her mouth, the bracelets vanished.

"Torrentia," the Queen said, "Don't even think about tricking me. Remember I possess the ClearSky Blade."

"But not one of you can wield it," Torrentia replied with a sly smile. "Save your empty threats. I will do as you asked, and you will not see me again."

Minutes later, a woman walked out of the cave, into the bright day. She hadn't seen sunlight in decades, and it took her eyes several seconds to adjust. She stretched her arms towards the sky, and her transformation began. Within seconds, the huge silver dragon was ready to take flight. Behind her, the Fairy Queen and her escorts stepped out of the cave.

"I hope I've done the right thing," the Queen said.

A group of four dragons, all of different colors, left a trail of destruction on their way to the Grand Oak Palace. They stopped as a winged shape flew over the top of the cliffs. A silver dragon swooped down in front of them, hovering in their faces. She wasn't quite as large as the other dragons, but she still had a presence that awed them. She hissed in dragon-speak, "Retreat! Return to the Dragonsands!"

Two of the dragons looked at each other, considering her words. Finally the green one answered, "We will not! Victory is in our grasp!"

"Then, die!" shouted the silver dragon, opening her mouth wide to show her wicked fangs. Faster than the dragons could follow, the silver dragon bit into the green dragon's neck. A blue dragon started to come to her rescue, when he was suddenly struck by a huge bolt of lightning. The silver dragon flew backward and muttered an incantation. The sky went black. Acid rain, massive hailstones, and rapid bolts of lightning all fell from the sky, bombarding all dragons present.

Torrentia, the Great WeatherWyrm of the Northlands, had decades of power stored up, and she loosed all of it on the dragon army. Those that weren't killed fled for their lives. When Torrentia was satisfied that she'd fulfilled her part of the bargain, she glared at the Grand Oak Palace, uttered a curse in dragon-speak, and flew off toward the Northern Regions.

The sun set, turning the world a furious orange as the day struggled to hold on to the light. The last of the surviving dragon invaders had long since retreated, and Torrentia was halfway back to her den in the north.

The Fairy Queen finally completed the last of the protection spells. She had worked hard on improving the Great Barrier, and was confident that this time there would be no counterspell. This time the Barrier could not be disrupted, circumvented, or avoided. Of course, that's what she'd said the last time.

Confident she'd done all she could, the Queen and her escorts teleported back to the palace. Many fairies would be working through the night collecting dragon blood and disposing of corpses. The next month would be a busy one for the entire fairy community. There were trees to replant, a garden to regrow, not to mention helping the Proudpath villagers with their damage. The Queen herself would have a full schedule inspecting their work. And of course, there would be a mass funeral for all those lost today. But things would return to normal, as they always did.

"Why would anyone want to be a brownie?" Honeycomb asked, struggling to pick up a wooden beam.

"That's not what I said," Thistle replied. "I said I am one." She flitted over to Honeycomb's side, helping her lift the beam.

"But you're clearly not," Honeycomb said. "You have wings. And glowy skin. And boobs."

"On the outside, yes," Thistle said. "But in here, I swear I was meant to be a brownie." She pointed to her head, causing her to lose her grip on the beam. She quickly put both hands back under the wood.

"Why though? Pixies are so much better. We can fly! And we have magic dust!" Working together Honeycomb and Thistle moved the beam to the side of the dirt road. They were about to grab another beam when they heard one of the villagers cry. They rushed over to see what the matter was.

"I can't stop the bleeding!" a woman cried. She was cradling a small boy, and using a piece of burlap to stanch a wound on his arm.

"Let me have a look," Honeycomb said. The villager looked afraid – she still wasn't used to the presence of the fey folk – but she let the pixie see. Honeycomb spread her fingers and said a few magic words. Glittering powder burst from her palm, landing on the child's arm. The wound glowed for a moment, then closed.

"Oh thank you!" the woman said, and hugged her child. The two pixies flew off, looking for more flotsam to clear.

"Let's see a brownie do that!" Honeycomb said.

"I know, I know," Thistle replied. "But you don't understand. I never said brownies were better than pixies. I didn't just wake up one morning and say, 'I wish I couldn't fly anymore.' But when I look at my reflection, I just look wrong to me. It's like I'm seeing someone else."

"Well, I think you're crazy," Honeycomb said, dragging a broken wagon wheel away from the road. "But that's probably why we get along so well. Do you want me to start calling you by a different name?"

"I haven't thought of one yet," Thistle replied, "But you'll be the first to know if I do."

"Tell me more about your kingdom," the old woman said. She'd been mortally wounded during the invasion, but she would live, thanks to Honeycomb's healing hands. Still, her recovery wasn't going to be a walk in the park. Magic could only do so much, and the greatest healers were back in the Fairy Kingdom, busy tending to their own wounded.

"What would you like to know?" Honeycomb asked, pouring some water into a wooden cup. Honeycomb looked like a young woman with blond hair, but she was less than a foot tall. Her transparent golden wings held her aloft as she flitted about the room, retrieving various salves and herbs.

"What's your name?" the woman asked.

"Honeycomb," she answered. "And this is Thistle," she added, gesturing toward her friend. It had been a long day, and most of the fairies had returned to their kingdom. Only Honeycomb and Thistle had remained behind to wrap up some loose ends.

"Beautiful names," the woman said. "I'm Amalla." She paused for a few moments, trying to decide what she wanted to ask first. Thistle pressed a wet rag to Amalla's forehead. Finally the old woman asked, "Are all of you girls?"

"Most of us," Thistle said.

"The sprites and pixies are girls," Honeycomb added. "Also the nixies and dryads. The grigs and brownies are boys, though."

"What's the difference between a pixie and a sprite?" Amalla asked.

"Sprites are smaller," Thistle said. "Like bug-sized. And kind of nuts."

"Thistle," Honeycomb said, stifling a laugh. It was true, though, just rude to point out.

"How do you... make more pixies?" Amalla asked. She was trying to ask a delicate question without offending them.

"Sex," Thistle said bluntly. "Surely you've heard of it?"

The old woman laughed at Thistle's brashness. Now that she knew she wasn't going to offend them, she was more frank herself. "So the pixies and sprites mate with the brownies and grigs?"

"Pretty much," Honeycomb confirmed. "Brownies have offspring with pixies or nixies. Sprites have offspring with grigs, 'cause they're smaller. Sometimes other pairings happen, thanks to magic and such."

Amalla kept asking questions, and the two answered as best they could while making her comfortable. They told her all about fairy society and biology. When she finally fell asleep, the two pixies gave some instructions to her caretaker, and flew back to the Fairy Kingdom. It was starting to rain.

Kra-koom! The Grand Oak Palace shook at the peal of thunder. A flash of lightning immediately followed, and for a moment, the Queen's bedroom was as bright as day. It had been raining since dusk, and the rainfall had grown heavier by the hour. Queen Delia rolled over and looked at the time. Across the room, a magical sundial sat on a stone pedestal, glowing throughout the night. It was well after midnight. She closed her eyes again, but another report sounded, even louder this time. The room shook, and a mirror tumbled off her dresser.

"Candlebright," the Queen said, and several candles lit up around the room. She tossed her spidersilk sheets aside and got to her feet. Then she reached for the thin dress hanging on her bedpost, and slipped it on over her head. She knelt and examined the shattered mirror. She'd once heard of a human superstition about broken mirrors and bad luck. While the fairies didn't share that fear, they had their own little rituals regarding shattered glass.

A mirror shattered by lightning became a powerful divination tool. It had to be an accident, however. The magic somehow "knew" if a mirror had been intentionally placed in the path of a storm. Not that it mattered in this case, as this mirror had been broken by thunder, not lightning. But was that close enough?

The mirror had fallen face down. As the Queen turned it over, for just a second, she saw a face that wasn't her own. Torrentia laughed at her from the broken shards, her face fractured and multiplied, a dozen sets of evil eyes fixing her with a triumphant glare. And then she was gone. Queen Delia didn't know if it had been her imagination or an actual portent.

The tree shook again, and this time the thunder and lightning came together. Five quick booms, each accompanied by blinding flashes of light. The Queen rose, backing away from her window. Three more crashes sounded, three more bursts of lightning. She heard yelling from outside her door, and quick footsteps. There was a knock at her door. They didn't wait for her to answer, but burst in.

"My Queen!" a brownie guard said. "We must get you to safety now!"

* * *

As the residents of Fairy Haven looked on in despair, the kingdom's largest oak became a lightning rod, struck over and over by angry fingers of electricity. It burst into flames, which burned despite the impossibly heavy downpour. The lighting strikes became stronger and more frequent, stabbing at the tree with sizzling knives, tearing it apart with claws of light. Within minutes, the grandest tree in the forest, which had stood for more than a thousand years, toppled to the ground.

From her enormous throne room in the Great Cavern of the Charred Mountain, the Dragon Queen Torrentia watched it all on her quartz scrying stone. She laughed maniacally, her face turning purple. Nearby, her two drake guards watched her uncomfortably, worried for her sanity.

The previous Dragon Queen, Lizbethia, still hung from enchanted manacles on the opposite wall. She'd ruled for more than fifty years, having taken over after Torrentia's capture. But she'd been no match for Torrentia's power, and the returning queen had made short work of her upon her arrival.

Both queens were currently in their human forms. Lizbethia was covered in horrific wounds, many of which would have been fatal to a lesser being. But she clung to life, dizzy, thirsty, her head pounding, her arms numb. The enchanted manacles would keep her alive, even as Lizbethia begged for death. She wouldn't heal, nor would she perish; she would simply remain in this near-death state for as long as Torrentia found it entertaining.

"If... you... wipe them out..." Lizbethia said, straining to speak, "You... won't have... dust..."

Torrentia thought on this. It was a good point. The dragons used fairy dust for certain spells and rituals, just as the fairies used dragon blood for some of theirs. It was the primary reason the dragons attempted to raid the Fairy

Kingdom. If not for the animosity between the two cultures, it could have been a symbiotic relationship.

"Well, they started it," Torrentia replied. She didn't know if it was true, but it's what she'd always been taught. The dragons and the fairies had been at war for centuries, and while no one could remember exactly how it had begun, both sides refused to take the blame. "They'll pay for those years I was locked up," Torrentia said. "I'll decide when they've had enough."

"But the nursery…" Lizbethia gasped. Torrentia knew what she meant. The dragon population was dwindling, mostly because they had a low birth rate. Dragon eggs required fairy dust to incubate. It was said that in ancient times, fairies and dragons had lived and worked together. Some even believed that the two species had created the world together, with the dragons carving out the mountains and rivers, while the fairies created the forests and animals.

Torrentia stood, walked over to Lizbethia, and stroked her chin. "Don't worry, Liz," she said. "I'm sure a few fairies will survive. They'll flee, regroup, start a new kingdom elsewhere. But they'll never question our superiority again." She turned back to her quartz stone. More bolts of lighting pounded at the fallen tree, and the fires were spreading through the forest.

Once again, Torrentia threw back her head and laughed.

"This one," Honeycomb said, pointing to a stump. Working together, Thistle and Honeycomb rolled the stump to the side, exposing a hole in the ground. A small swarm of sprites emerged from the hole, thanking the two pixies for freeing them. The hole was nearly flooded; they'd arrived just in time.

It was daybreak, though you could barely tell due to the heavy storm clouds. The lightning had let up a bit since the fall of the Grand Oak, but the rain was just as strong as it had been all night. Honeycomb thought about the human village nearby. Were they getting flooded? They were still recovering from one disaster, another this soon was just too much. But Honeycomb forced herself to let go of these thoughts; she had her own people to think about right now.

The pixies were covered in mud, not to mention splinters and cuts. They couldn't fly in the pounding rain, so they'd had to search for survivors on foot. They were also running low on magic fairy dust. "This must be what it's like to be a human," Honeycomb said, digging through some fallen branches. Her muscles ached, and she wished she could sit down and rest a bit. "Or a brownie," she added, glancing pointedly at Thistle.

Thistle just shrugged, pulling aside a large branch. In addition to being landbound, brownies couldn't generate fairy dust. Sure, they could cast spells, but not innately. They had to study to use magic, same as any human wizard. If Thistle ever, somehow, got her wish, she'd be giving up a lot. But again, it wasn't a want, it just... was. Walking around on two feet, using her muscle more than her spells, it felt right to her, somehow. She was tired and bleeding, but right now she felt more like herself than she had in a long time.

Pushing aside a large rock, they uncovered the entrance to a grig den. These poor grigs had not been as lucky as the sprites. The den was completely flooded, and several lifeless bodies floated on the surface of the water.

There was no time to mourn. The two pixies rushed to the next pile of detritus, looking for more survivors.

Nearly two hundred brownies crowded into the cavern, and more were on the way. The line led to a simple table, on top of which lay a sword. Queen Delia stood behind the table, clearing her throat. She'd spent all night on the run. She was wet, cold, and injured, but there was no time for rest now. Every minute she hesitated, more would die.

She looked terrible. Her clothing was in tatters, her hair was full of twigs, and one of her wings was broken. But her audience still gave her the same reverence as always, and became completely silent when she tried to speak.

"Thank you for coming," the Queen said, and then went into a coughing fit. Three sprites carried over a wooden cup full of warm honey nectar. While the Queen drank it, another sprite touched the Queen's throat, which glowed for a moment. This annoyed the Queen, but she didn't say anything. She'd been waving off healers all morning. She wanted her healing sprites out in the kingdom, helping survivors.

"I know many of you would rather be out helping your loved ones, and I'm sorry to keep you," the Queen said. "But this is a matter that takes precedence over all else. Fifty years ago, Torrentia was captured using the ClearSky Blade. The wielder was mortally wounded in the fight, and he will forever be remembered as a hero."

She took another drink. "It is said that Torrentia can only be killed by another silver dragon, but it's also said that she's the last of her kind. The ClearSky Blade was forged from the tooth of a silver dragon, and it is believed to be the only weapon in existence that can defeat her." She gestured toward the blade, but didn't touch it.

"The blade holds a powerful curse. It can't be wielded by anyone but a brownie, as even touching the hilt will kill most fairies. Even brownies can't hold it for long, as it causes them horrendous pain until they pass out. Only one brownie in a generation can wield it properly. The chosen one."

She cleared her throat, and took another sip of nectar. "That's why you're here. Some of you have tried to wield the blade before, but perhaps this time you'll—" She coughed some more, and the sprites brought her a fresh drink.

When she spoke again, she sounded less regal, and more desperate. "This has to work," she said. "The storm will continue until it wipes us out, unless we kill her. One of you *has* to be this generation's chosen one. Whichever of you manages to defeat Torrentia, you will forever be known as a hero. In addition, you will become my new king."

The brownies lined up in front of the sword. As the first one approached, the Queen's attendant announced his name. "Curloyle Verdane," she said, looking into a small crystal ball. Curloyle nodded respectfully to the Queen, then reached for the sword. He gripped the hilt, and attempted to lift the blade. He tried to look triumphant as he held the sword aloft, but he couldn't hide the pain in his eyes. Curloyle collapsed to the floor and crawled away, the sword clattering at the feet of the next brownie in line.

"This is a dumb idea," Honeycomb said.

"I have to try," Thistle said, donning a robe. With her wings flat against her back, the heavy cloth made it difficult to tell she was a pixie. Her face and hair were filthy from all their rescue work, which helped the illusion.

Honeycomb shook her head. "The blade will kill you."

"So will not knowing," Thistle countered. "This is just something I have to do."

Honeycomb nodded. "I understand. Well, no, not really. But I know you, and I know you have to be you."

Thistle leaned forward and kissed her on the lips. They felt sparks between them; actual, visible sparks, the kind that only appear when fated fey couples kiss. They should have been surprised at the revelation, but it felt so right, that neither questioned it.

"I hope you find out what you need to know," Honeycomb said as she pulled away.

Thistle just nodded. She pulled her hood up over her head, and began walking toward the cavern.

Honeycomb watched her go, worried that it might be the last time she saw her.

* * *

No one questioned the robed brownie with the obscured face. Everyone in line was disheveled and in various states of dress, and besides, their attention was on the sword, not the crowd. It wasn't until Thistle was tenth in line that she realized she might be in trouble. One of the Queen's attendants, a pixie wearing the robes of a seer, held a crystal orb. As each brownie approached, she called out their name.

I'm going to get in so much trouble, Thistle thought, looking around nervously. She considered making a break for it, but she had to see this through. She wondered if she'd be sentenced to hard labor. But for what crime? Trying to save the kingdom? The Queen was too busy with the current crisis to start throwing out punishments for no reason. *Besides*, Thistle thought, *If the sword rejects me, I won't survive long enough to get punished.*

She watched as the brownies in front of her each tried to wield the blade, only to drop it, shrieking in pain. Finally it was her turn. The sword sat before her, halfway off the table from where the previous brownie had dropped it.

"Thistletta Rosebush," the attendant said aloud, then did a double take.

The Queen looked at Thistle strangely. "Please remove your hood," she said.

Thistle complied, revealing her face to the shocked Queen. "Please let me try," Thistle begged.

"I know you want to help," Queen Delia said. "But it will kill you. I'm sorry, but you'll have to leave."

Thistle nodded, and started to turn away. Then she stopped, rushed to the table, and grabbed the hilt before anyone could stop her.

Queen Torrentia was growing bored. The scrying stone continued to show scenes of violent weather. But the fey folk had taken refuge in caves, where Torrentia's storms couldn't reach them. Sure, there was some entertainment value in watching their treehouses topple and their gardens flood, but the best part was over. The Queen had gone underground, beyond the reach of Torrentia's scrying stone.

She passed the time by throwing daggers at Lizbethia. The woman couldn't die, but she could still scream in pain whenever a dagger hit a particularly tender spot. Whenever she ran out of daggers, a drake servant would pluck them out of Lizbethia, and return them to a box at Torrentia's side. But even this was getting boring. The Dragon Queen considered finishing Lizbethia off, but she knew it was something she could only do once, and didn't want to lose her favorite toy. She decided she'd wait until the Fairy Queen was in her custody. Oh yes, she would make a fine replacement.

"My Queen," said a drake guard, shaking Torrentia out of her reverie. She glared at the interruption, but nodded for him to continue. "We have visitors," he said. "Representatives from the Fairy Kingdom wish to negotiate."

Torrentia laughed out loud. "Negotiate," she repeated, twisting the word with her tongue. "This should be fun. Is the Queen with them?"

"No," the guard said. "Two pixies, and four brownie guards. And they've brought the blade."

"The ClearSky blade?" she asked incredulously. The guard nodded. "Make the brownies wait outside," Torrentia said. She couldn't take the chance. "But send in the pixies. Let's see what they have to say. This should be fun."

The guard nodded and walked away. A few minutes later, he returned with the two pixies. They carried a large, folded leaf, which was wrapped around a sword.

"A gift, for me?" Torrentia asked, her eyes on the sword.

Both pixies bowed. "Queen Torrentia Wyvernica Demonicus," one said, "I am Honeycomb Leafwillow, and this is Thistletta Rosebush. We've been sent by Queen Delia to negotiate. If you will end the curse plaguing our kingdom, we offer you the ClearSky Blade."

"My, my, the Queen must be desperate indeed, to part with such a rare weapon," Torrentia said. "Or maybe she realized it was useless to her, since none of you can wield it."

"Nevertheless, it is yours," Thistle said. "You just have to remove your curse."

"Very well, I accept," Torrentia said. She had no intention of ending the curse, but these two didn't need to know that. Once she had the sword, she would slay these visitors and punish the Fairy Kingdom even more. She nodded toward the sword, and held out her hand.

Thistle flew forward until she hovered just a few feet away from the Dragon Queen. She unwrapped the leaf, but rather than hand over the sword, she grabbed it by the hilt. Thistle now assumed a battle pose, and glared at the evil queen. "This is your last chance," Thistle said. "End the curse, or I will end your life."

Torrentia's expression didn't change, but she did take a step back. "That must be a fake," she said. "No pixie can wield that weapon."

"I'm no ordinary pixie," Thistle said. "But if you don't believe your eyes, I'll be happy to give you a demonstration." She swiped the sword through the air a few times, leaving faint blue lines in the air. Though the pixie was dwarfed by the Torrentia's human form, Thistle showed no fear, and returned the Dragon Queen's glare with fire in her eyes.

For just a moment, a visage of fear crossed Torrentia's face. But then she laughed, shaking her head slowly. Something changed in the room. The air itself seemed to come alive with energy. "You may hold the weapon," she said. "But do you have the skill to use it in battle? I think not."

"Try me," Thistle said. She kept a brave face, but she could feel the hair rising on her neck.

"Be careful what you wish for," Torrentia said, then

suddenly thrust her hand forward. A blast of electricity flew from her fingertips, a bolt every bit as powerful as the ones that had toppled the Great Palace. The room flashed with blinding blue light, and even Torrentia had to blink a few times before she could see again.

Thistle remained where she'd been, hovering a few feet away. Her blade now glowed bright blue, with sparks of electricity popping and crackling around it.

Torrentia opened her mouth to say something, but no words came out. "Guards," she finally managed to squeak. "Kill them."

Thistle pointed her sword at one of the guards. A bolt of lightning blasted him, leaving nothing but a smoking corpse. The remaining guards turned and fled.

"Traitors!" Torrentia shouted. Then, to Thistle, she said, "Maybe we can negotiate after all. I'll draw up a peace treaty. Just let me go get my pen." Then she turned and ran.

A jolt of lightning hit her in the back, and she tumbled onto her face. As she got to her knees, her head turned toward Thistle, her face contorted with fury. As the pixies watched, she grew, doubling in size, then tripling, her silver dress merging with her skin, covering her in shiny scales. When the transformation was complete, she filled the cavern, her head nearly touching the high ceiling. The silver dragon stared at Thistle with contempt, and let loose with her lightning breath.

The air crackled around Thistle, and it was hard to breathe, but the sword continued to protect her. She could feel the weapon's power growing in her hands, and the energy seemed to flow through her body. Her blood felt like it was boiling, but she felt no pain, only power. She let loose the blade's energy, firing a blast so powerful the ground shook.

Torrentia was sent flying across the cave, where she hit the wall hard. That burst of energy would have turned a lesser dragon into ash, but she managed to shrug it off.

"Fine," she said, in a deep, gravelly voice, "We'll do this the hard way." She leapt forward with surprising speed, and attempted to bite the pixie. Thistle just barely got out of the way in time. The two fought back and forth, Torrentia dodging the pixie's stabs, and Thistle keeping away from those mighty jaws.

Honeycomb watched from across the room. She wanted to help her friend, but she had no weapon that could harm the dragon. She heard a groan to her right, where Lizbethia still hung from her magical chains, several daggers protruding from her body. Honeycomb debated for a few seconds, then approached the former dragon queen.

"Ow!" Thistle shouted, as the dragon backhanded her across the room. She hit the wall, then tumbled to the ground. She rolled to the side just as a massive foot stomped beside her. Not wanting to waste the opportunity, Thistle stabbed Torrentia in the foot. The silver dragon roared in pain, withdrawing her foot.

As powerful as the ClearSky blade was, Thistle still had her work cut out for her. The blade protected her from lightning, which was a lifesaver, but its blasts weren't powerful enough to penetrate the dragon's scales. And while it was the only weapon capable of piercing Torrentia's hide, Thistle was having a devil of a time hitting anything vital. The dragon was unbelievably fast, and it stayed on the offensive. Thistle barely had time to dodge the creature's bites, much less find a weak spot to target.

Torrentia let loose another breathful of lightning, and Thistle barely brought the sword up in time to block it. Then the dragon spun, whipping her massive tail at the pixie, once again knocking her against the wall. Thistle got to her knees, dazed from the impact. Her sword had clattered away somewhere to her left, but she kept her eyes on her enemy. She was seeing double, and she had to blink a couple of times before she could tell which dragon was the real one.

Except they were both real. The silver one charged

toward her, but the purple one stood still. "Torrentia!" the newcomer bellowed, and the silver dragon turned.

"Lizbethia," Torrentia growled. "How did you get loose?"

"We have a new treaty with the fairies," Lizbethia replied, nodding toward Honeycomb. "If you wish to avoid execution, you will surrender immediately."

Torrentia chuckled, a noise that sounded like an avalanche. "That is not within your power," she said. "But if you want the throne, come and take it." As if to hammer home the threat with a visual aid, she reached forward and grasped her human-sized throne, snapping it off its dais.

The purple dragon screeched and rushed forward, her fangs going for Torrentia's neck. The two wrestled, causing the cavern to shake. Honeycomb watched the fight in awe. It was like being witness to a battle between gods, the kind of match that could reshape the world if it went on long enough.

The titanic reptiles tossed each other against the walls, rocks falling with every impact. Finally Torrentia got her jaws around Lizbethia's neck. Just as she was about to bite, she cried out in pain. She turned her head to see Thistle standing on her back, the ClearSky Blade buried hilt deep between the silver scales. It wasn't a lethal wound, but it hurt more than anything Torrentia had ever felt. She released Lizbethia and moved her head towards the pixie, her massive jaws open wide.

And then Thistle released the blade's electricity. Still buried in the dragon's skin, the lightning flowed through Torrentia's body, burning her from the inside. The silver dragon wailed, an unholy, ear-splitting shriek that echoed throughout the cavern. Smoke rose from her mouth, and her eyes burst like overripe melons. Finally her head hit the floor, and her breathing stopped.

Lizbethia reverted to her human form, and Honeycomb sprinkled fairy dust on her wounds. The three headed back toward the cavern entrance, so they could inform the drakes of the change in leadership. The drakes were more than happy to follow Lizbethia again, as she'd been a much kinder master in their eyes.

The brownie guards were let into the cavern, and the drakes set up a table where the visiting fairies could parley with the new Dragon Queen. "A flying brownie, I thought I'd seen everything," Queen Lizbethia said, studying Thistle with admiration.

"I'm just a pixie," Thistle said, her voice tinged with disappointment. "I don't know why the blade chose me."

Lizbethia shook her head, and her eyes glowed for a moment. "You only see things as they are," she said. "I see things as they were meant to be. You have the soul of a brownie, make no mistake about that."

"You really think so?" Thistle asked.

The Dragon Queen nodded. "Tell me," she asked. "If you could transform, so that your body matched your mind, would you?"

"In a heartbeat," Thistle said. "But no such spell exists."

"Maybe not that *you* know of," Lizbethia replied with a wry smile.

One month later, there was a celebration in the village of Proudpath. The townsfolk had prepared a banquet in the center of town, and everyone feasted together – humans, fey folk, and even Lizbethia, in her human form. Queen Delia sat next to her, the two still hammering out the details of their trade agreement.

Honeycomb and Thistle sat next to each other, locked in intense conversation, barely even noticing the world around them. Thistle was completely a brownie now, from head to toe, and he'd never been happier. The transformation spell had used a combination of fairy dust and dragon blood – Torrentia's blood, to be precise – and the change was permanent. Thistle felt like he was finally experiencing life for the first time, instead of just watching the world through someone else's eyes.

The Fairy Queen had offered Thistle the throne, but he'd turned it down. He'd experienced a rebirth, and he didn't want to waste this new life writing decrees and ordering people around. Besides, he didn't want to have to marry the Queen. While Queen Delia would certainly make an ideal partner – she was intelligent, beautiful, and full of grace – Thistle's heart already belonged to another, and he stared into her eyes now.

Sparks flew again as Thistle and Honeycomb kissed. The rest of the table seemed to fade away, the sounds of raucous celebration becoming a distant hum. Their kiss was so strong, their connection so intimate, that they could feel each other's heartbeats. For just a moment, Thistle believed he could even hear Honeycomb's thoughts.

Life wasn't back to normal, and things might never be the same again. Rebuilding the Fairy Kingdom would take months if not years. There were other dragon factions, beyond Lizbethia's control. And dragons weren't the only monsters out there.

But right now, at least for Thistle and Honeycomb, the world was as perfect as it ever would be.

Hero Worship

"That's not your real hair color, is it?" It came out more accusatory than I meant it. I didn't care if she colored her hair. Half the people in the club had dyed hair, some in colors that didn't exist in nature. I was just trying to keep the conversation going, and I'd already complimented her freckles twice.

But if she was offended, she didn't show it. "What gave it away?" she asked with an amused smile.

"Hard to say," I answered, nearly shouting to be heard above the thump-thump-thumping music. "Don't get me wrong, I like the black, but it doesn't seem to go with your skin tone."

"Should I have gone blonde?" she asked. Her accent didn't really match her face, either, but I'm not really sure what I mean by that. Her face looked... well, I'm not good with faces, maybe Irish? But her melodious voice didn't sound like anything I'd heard before. Wherever she was from, I could have listened to her talk all day, and I found myself wishing we'd agreed to meet somewhere less noisy.

"I think you'd look good with any hair color," I said. No! Too much! It wasn't even the kind of thing I'd normally say, especially to someone I'd just met. But she was so captivating, my brain had stopped working. I expected her to stand up and walk out right then. She had to know she was out of my league.

She laughed. "Thank you," she said. "Your nice is hair, too. I mean, your hair's nice." And then, for just a second, she cringed at what she'd said. *She* cringed. This goddess actually cared what I thought of her.

"Where is your voice from?" I asked, then nearly rolled my eyes at my own phrasing. "Your accent, I mean."

"I was born in London, but I've lived in five different countries," she said. "And you?"

"I'm a local," I said. "Born and raised in Gantua City. I've never lived more than ten miles from the house I grew up in. I've never even been out of the country. Oh god, you've got to think I'm so boring."

She laughed again, and I swear I thought I heard angels singing. "My parents moved around," she said. "That doesn't make me interesting. I've had to make new friends so often, eventually I gave up. I barely know how to talk to people anymore."

I could relate to that. "You?" I said, and she nodded. "God, look at you. Guys had to be lining up to talk to you."

"They did," she admitted. "But they didn't want to be my friend, they just wanted, well, you know. And I didn't want that from them."

I nodded, and tried to think of a clever reply.

"Let me ask you a question," she said. "Is this really your scene?" She gestured around the club. Beyond our table, women danced to the oontz-oontz-oontz of a techno beat. The flashing lights were already giving me a headache.

"Not really," I said. "It just seemed like a safe place to meet." The ScisR app was just for women, but you could never be too careful. The fact that I'd matched with such a knockout only made me that much more suspicious. Even here in real life, Kat looked exactly like the kind of fake profile picture a man might use to trick someone.

But nevertheless, we were hitting it off. For the next twenty minutes, we talked about our jobs, movies, and video games. It turned out we had a lot in common. I was starting to think we'd be leaving in one car.

"So, is Kat short for Katherine, or…" I started to say, before I was drowned out by screams and gunfire. I looked towards the entrance in shock, but I couldn't see through the crowd.

"Get under the table!" Kat ordered, and her voice was so authoritative, my body replied before my brain had even processed the request. Under the table, Kat looked me in the eyes and thrust her purse into my hands. "Stay here," she said, pulling off her wig.

Her real hair was close-cropped and bright red. If not for the circumstances, I might have said, "I knew it!" As it was, I just stared wide-eyed with my mouth open. What happened next only stunned me even more.

Kat's face became blank and smooth, as a mirror-like sheen spread across her body. In a half second she was completely featureless, a woman-shaped silver mannequin, reminiscent of the evil robot in that Schwarzenegger movie. And then she was gone, off to confront whatever madman was terrorizing the club.

Of course I'd heard of Kromia. I'd lost track of the number of superheroes protecting our globe, but I tried to keep up with the ones active in my city. This wasn't even the first time I'd seen a superhero in person. But it was definitely the first time I'd been on a date with one.

I didn't get to see her fight with the shooter. There were too many people in the way, and I stayed hidden under the table. When the police announced the all-clear, I followed the crowd out into the rain. I'd parked two blocks away, but I don't remember the walk. I was in shock, and my body moved on its own. It wasn't until I reached the car that I snapped out of it. My keys wouldn't open the car door. It was a puzzle I couldn't solve on autopilot, and my consciousness slapped itself awake.

These weren't my keys. But I'd gotten them from my

purse? And then I realized I was carrying two purses. I was holding a superhero's purse. I had been on a date with a superhero. I'd almost hooked up with a superhero. It was enough to send my brain buzzing, but then I remembered the tragedy I'd just witnessed. It was all too much. I got dizzy. I probably shouldn't have been driving, but I needed to get home.

I entered my apartment and locked the door. I didn't feel safe enough, so I wedged a chair under the doorknob. Then I turned on all the lights, making sure no one else was there. I even checked that little closet with the water heater. I wasn't usually this paranoid, but I'd just had a not-so-nice reminder that we live in a dangerous world.

I felt like I'd washed down a bottle of sleeping pills with an entire pot of coffee. My body wanted to crash, but I knew I wasn't going to get a wink of sleep tonight. I collapsed on the couch, and set the purses down next to me. I turned on the TV and put it on a news channel. I didn't really want to relive the scene yet, but the need for more details gnawed at the corners of my mind. The report was live, and police were still at the club. They said there were several injuries, but no deaths had been reported so far. The shooter was alive and in police custody.

While the first shots had been fired from a handgun, the shooter had also carried an automatic rifle. According to witnesses, he'd been in the process of switching out guns when Kromia stopped him. If she hadn't been there...

It occurred to me that my dating life had saved lives. I laughed out loud. It wasn't really that funny, but all my emotions were set to maximum. I laughed until I cried, then I ran to the bathroom and threw up. Once I had that out of my system, I finally started to pull myself together.

I remembered the purse. Kat's purse. She'd need that back. I didn't have her number, so I'd have to contact her through the ScisR app. Set up another "safe" place to meet. I didn't even know her last name.

"Idiot," I admonished myself. I tried to slap my forehead but I just ended up poking myself in the eye. Okay, I wasn't completely back together yet. I half-stumbled, half-crawled back to the living room, sat on the floor in front of the couch, and pulled Kat's purse down to me. I rooted through the purse, oddly amazed at the mundane items it contained. I'm not sure what I was expecting, maybe magic rocks or something. But no, just pens, phone, gum, keys, tampons, the usual stuff. I'd never specifically wondered if superheroes had periods, but now I knew.

I found her license in a side pocket, along with a few credit cards and some cash. God, even her driver's license photo was stunning, how did she do that? Her full name was Katrina Campbell. I looked at her address. I didn't recognize the street name, but it was here in Gantua city. I could return the purse in person, if I wanted. I pictured myself knocking on her door and handing the purse over, maybe with a bouquet of flowers.

"Eep!" I shouted, the license fumbling out of my hands as her phone vibrated. I picked it up and answered it. "H... hello?"

"Erin?" I recognized the voice right away. I could never forget that voice.

"That's me," I said sheepishly.

"Good, you still have it," Kat said. "Can I come over and get my purse?"

"Of course!" I said, and recited my address without thinking.

"You haven't told anyone who I am, have you?"

Wow. What a question. I'd seen this trope in movies all my life. The villain would ask, "Have you told anyone else?" right before capping a witness. I wasn't sure what to say. If I said yes, she'd be mad that I exposed her secret. If I said no, she could kill me and be satisfied there were no more loose ends. But it didn't matter. I don't think I could have lied to her if I'd tried. "No," I said. "And I won't, I promise."

"Thank goodness," she said. "I'll be right there." The call ended.

It wasn't until I put her phone back in her purse that I started having second thoughts. What if she thought I knew too much? Surely a superhero wouldn't resort to murder to protect her identity. But how would I know? Maybe there are no real heroes. Maybe all power corrupts, and the heroes only save lives to keep up appearances. Kromia might have a stash of bodies hidden in a volcano somewhere, people who discovered her secret identity, criminals she didn't feel like taking to the police, or maybe even people who cut her off in traffic.

No, the woman I talked to at the club would never do that. I know I'd talked to her for less than half an hour, but I couldn't picture beautiful-but-socially-awkward Kat killing anyone. Would she? She wouldn't be the first killer to hide behind a socially-inept persona. I considered finding a weapon, just to be safe. Yeah, right. Just a couple of hours ago, she took out a guy with an automatic rifle, and I expected to protect myself with a kitchen knife?

"Eep!" I shrieked again, as I heard a knock on the door. Except it wasn't the front door, but the balcony. I pulled the curtain aside, and Kromia was standing there on the other side of the glass door, her silver skin reflecting the light from my living room lamp. She waved awkwardly. I unlatched the door and slid it open.

"Is that too cliché?" she asked. "Showing up on your balcony? I saw it in a movie once and had to do it. It was smarmy, wasn't it." She covered her mirrored face with her hands.

And that's when I knew I was safe. I don't know a lot about murderers, but I'm pretty sure they don't obsess over sappy entrances. "It was great," I assured her. "Come on in."

"Thanks," she said, following me into the living room. I bent down to retrieve her things.

Kromia's silver sheen faded, and she looked human again. Her hair was still short and red, which reminded me of something. "Sorry," I said, handing over her purse. "I didn't grab the wig."

"That's okay," she laughed. "I didn't expect you to, and I have more wigs. I mainly wanted my phone and cards. It's such a hassle to replace them. Thank you so much for holding onto them."

It suddenly hit me that I was talking to a superhero. In my own living room. And she seemed to like me. I stared into her face for a little too long.

"I guess… I'll be going?" she said.

"You saved a lot of lives tonight," I said. "Probably even mine."

Kat looked sad. "I guess so. I was in the right place at the right time. But there's sickos like that all over the world, and I can't always be there to stop them. It's not like I have super speed. I mostly just fly around and punch people."

I stepped forward and put a hand on her shoulder. "You saved *my* life," I said, and leaned in to kiss her. She didn't turn away, but she didn't kiss back either. "Sorry," I said, pulling away. "I thought there was a spark."

"There is," she said, looking into my eyes. "But I don't want to kiss a gushing fan. I want to kiss the woman I was with at the club, the one who likes roleplaying games and cheesy rom-coms. I want you to like me as a person, not because I saved your life." She started to turn toward the balcony again.

"Wait," I said. "Can you stay for a while?"

"Are you asking Kat or… Kromia?" She put her hands on her hips at that last word, striking a heroic pose.

"Kat," I said. "If you stay, I promise I won't even mention Kromia. We'll watch a movie, maybe order a pizza…"

And just like that, her arms were around me. "Of course I'll stay," she said into my ear. Her breath sent shivers up and down my spine. As she started to pull away, I kissed her again. This time she kissed back. Her breath smelled minty. Sometime between the club and my balcony, she'd stopped to brush her teeth.

The one kiss became several, and soon the two of us devolved into a tempest of hungry hands and eager lips, each desperate to explore all that the other had to offer. We left a trail of discarded clothing to my bedroom, like breadcrumbs left by soon-to-be-lost children.

We never got around to watching that movie.

The next morning I woke up next to another person for the first time since moving into this apartment. We showered – together – then had breakfast. After another hour in the bedroom, doing... things, Kat had to leave for work. We agreed to meet up later, after her shift was over.

It's been ten years since the Vigilante Certification Act was signed into national law, and now superheroes have scheduled hours just like police officers. They're still encouraged to save lives when a disaster is happening right in front of them, such as the shooting at the club, but they can't go looking for trouble. In any emergency, whether on the clock or not, they're required to stick to their priorities: Saving lives and neutralizing danger. An unarmed criminal is no longer a threat, and therefore no longer the hero's responsibility. Gone are the days when "dark and edgy" antiheroes beat villains to a pulp; now the goal was to disarm and restrain.

Today, Kromia would be helping the police with follow-up procedures from the club shooting. Any hours left in her shift would be spent at the Hero Dispatch Center, waiting for something bad to happen.

I, however, had the day off. I had planned to spend the day tidying up the place, then maybe going to the gym. But after the club and the night of passion – wow, I actually had a night of passion, I still couldn't believe it – I couldn't focus on anything. I did start cleaning up, but my mind was elsewhere. My body moved of its own accord, loading the dishwasher, gathering up the dirty laundry, vacuuming, all while a million thoughts swirled through my head like bees in a tornado.

What if I'd matched with someone else? How many would have died? Would I have been among them?

What if Kat and I got married? Would it be like marrying a cop? Would I have to worry that she might not make it home every night?

I wanted to get Kat a present. What would she like? The very least I could do was plan the perfect date. I'd take her to the nicest restaurant I knew. I'd have to check my credit card balances first, but I was sure I had some room on one of them.

When I finally shook myself from my reverie, I realized I was mopping the kitchen floor. When did that happen? I didn't even remember filling the mop bucket. I finished the job and looked around the apartment. It was sparkling. I have a lot of quirks, some more useful than others. Nervous cleaning is one of the better ones.

All that was left was laundry. I'd have to go to the basement for that. I still wasn't keen on leaving my apartment, but at least I wasn't going into public. As I locked my door, I saw a man down the hall. He was leaning against the wall, looking at his phone. He glanced up for half a second, then went back to his phone.

There was nothing unusual about his behavior, but it still put me on edge. I wasn't sure if he was giving me a creepy vibe, or if last night had made me suspicious of everyone I saw. Fortunately I didn't have to walk in his direction. Basket under my arm, I turned the opposite way and took the stairs down to the laundry room.

The laundry room was empty. Two of the machines were running, but there were still plenty of empty ones, and I was only doing one load. I shoved my clothes into one of the machines. As I shut the door, I saw my reflection in the clear window. There was a man behind me. The same man from upstairs. I started to turn around, but everything went black.

I dreamed about Kat, only I was the superhero and she was the damsel in distress. In the dream, she kept falling off of things. Buildings, airplanes, cliffs… and each time I had to fly down to save her. But I couldn't fly faster than she fell, so she always remained mere inches from my grasp, both of us hurtling downward. Each time she neared the ground, the scene faded, and we were whisked away to another scenario. On the last one, she was falling off my own apartment building. The fall seemed to last for hours, as I flew past dozens, hundreds, thousands of floors in my futile efforts to reach her.

My nose itched. I tried to scratch it, but I couldn't make my hands move toward my nose. Despite my life-or-death pursuit of Kat's falling form, the itch became my focus. We stopped falling, and just floated in the air while I tried to figure out why I couldn't reach my own nose. The itch was the only thing that felt real anymore, and trying to figure it out woke me from the dream.

I opened my eyes, and saw the city skyline. It was nighttime again; I'd missed most of the day. My hands were above my head, bound by rope, in a position similar to how I'd been flying in the dream. I dangled from some scaffolding, nothing below my feet, swinging slightly with the wind. I could feel something heavy strapped to my back. The wind blew my hair across my face, tickling my nose. I couldn't figure out where I was. This seemed weirder than the dream.

My mind was in overdrive. Looking at the skyline, I was able to work out where I was in relation to downtown. Looking below, I recognized my favorite bookstore, and realized what street I was on. I also nearly lost my lunch, and had to close my eyes again to shut out the vertigo. I knew where I was now. I'd driven past this half-built building dozens of times. I was starting to wonder if it would ever be finished.

I heard some movement to my right. I turned my head and risked opening my eyes. As long as I didn't look down, I could tolerate the height. My abductor stood on a wooden platform. He was now wearing a garish suit, with a plaid jacket and tie, in bright shades of green and blue. He held a microphone in one hand, and he looked at me with a plastic grin.

"Good, you're awake," he said, his microphone amplifying his voice above the wind. "The show will start soon. I'm just waiting for the other contestant to arrive." He stressed nearly every word in each sentence, with the over-the-top flair of a circus ringmaster.

"Who are you?" I asked, but I don't think he heard me. He kept testing his mic, and making adjustments to a speaker behind him.

"And heeeere sheee comes!" he exclaimed. I realized it wasn't ringmaster he was going for, but rather…

My thought was interrupted as Kromia flew into view. She came to a stop, hovering a few feet away from me, her attention on the villain.

"Not so fast," he said, his finger hovering over one of three large buttons on the side of his microphone. "One wrong move and she dies!"

"Are you okay?" Kromia asked, briefly turning towards me. I started to answer, but I was drowned out by the bad guy's spiel.

"The contestants are in place, and now it's time to play 'Win or Die Trying!' I'm your host, Captain Gameshow!" Even though we were the only two people who could see him, the guy acted as if he had an audience of thousands, bowing in every direction before continuing.

"I'm not here to play your sadistic games!" Kromia shouted.

The villain was unfazed. "I'm afraid the game isn't

optional. If you don't play, she dies. If you lose, she dies. If you attack me, she dies. If I drop this mic, she dies. But if you play and win, she goes free. " He still overemphasized every word, playing up to the imaginary crowd, and the schtick was already getting old.

"Fine," Kromia said. "What are the rules?"

"I will give you a list of seven tasks, much like the labors of Theseus." The dude didn't even get the mythology right. He started rattling off a list of tasks for Kromia to perform. Some were illegal, some were humiliating, some were dangerous. Among other things, she was required to break some of his friends out of prison, to rob a bank and hand over the money, to reveal her secret identity to the world, and she even had to dance naked on live TV.

But I only heard bits and pieces of the rules, because I was busy with a Herculean task of my own. I refused to be a pawn in some stupid game, and I wasn't about to let Kat end her superhero career just to save a nobody like me. While Gameshow's attention was focused on Kromia, I concentrated on my bonds.

I'm no superhero, but everybody's got a talent. Six years ago I was in a car wreck, and I broke several bones in my left hand. Ever since then, I've been able to dislocate my thumb at will. Though I was scared out of my wits, I managed to wriggle my left hand free of the rope. But now what? Maybe I could use my left hand to undo the right, but that would mean falling to my death.

Earlier I'd noticed a strange weight on my back, and now that I could feel around, I was able to figure it out. I was wearing a backpack. I felt my way down the straps, hoping for… yes! The straps were attached with belt clips, which were easily unfastened. There was a third strap around my waist, which was just as easy to remove. The bad guy had probably counted on the fact that I wouldn't be able to use my hands, or he would have found a more secure way to strap the backpack onto me.

I undid the one at the waist first, then the one across my left shoulder. As I unclipped the final strap, Gameshow noticed what I was up to. "Hey, stop that!" he shouted. He pressed the button on the microphone, but it was too late. The backpack was halfway to the ground when it exploded. It wasn't a huge blast, but I still felt the heat blow past me. If it had detonated a few floors higher, I might have lost a foot. The scaffolding shook, and hanging from the rope as I was, I was tossed around like a tetherball.

With his only leverage neutralized, Gameshow shrieked and dropped his microphone. He started to draw a handgun from inside his jacket, but Kromia was on him in an instant. She punched him in the face, knocking him out cold.

The scaffolding creaked and groaned, then started to topple. Kromia threw Gameshow over her shoulder, then flew toward me. She caught me, but my right hand was still tied to the rope. The scaffolding collapsed, yanking me right out of her arms. I don't even know what happened next. I hurtled toward the ground, face first, but all I could see was darkness and dust.

You ever have one of those dreams where you're falling, and you wake up right before you hit the ground? I had the opposite experience. I passed through the dust cloud, saw the pavement approaching fast, and blacked out.

Fighting my way out of a dream where I was on a deadly game show – wow, new fear unlocked – I gradually became aware of a beeping sound. The game show vanished in a vortex of darkness. In its place, a truck began backing towards me, the pulsing beeps warning me to get out of the way. I tried to move, but my feet were rooted to the ground, held in place by swirls of darkness. I tried waving my arms, but the driver couldn't see me. "Please don't hit me," I said aloud.

"No one's going to hit you," came Kat's melodic voice. "You're safe now."

Her voice pulled me out of the darkness, and I opened my eyes. I was in a hospital bed. The beeping came from a machine to my right. To my left, Kat stood by my bedside, looking at me with concern.

"What happened?" I asked.

"What do you remember?" she asked.

My memories were a jumbled mess, but I managed to pick out the finer points. "The backpack exploded, and I fell."

"You didn't just fall," Kat said. "That rope pulled you, and dislocated your shoulder. I managed to free you before you hit the ground, but you still got hit by some falling debris. The doctors were worried you might have a concussion. Your wrist has seen better days, too."

I looked at my bandaged arm. I didn't feel any pain at the moment, and I wondered what meds they had me on. "How long was I out?" I asked. It was still dark outside the window.

"Just a few hours," she said. "It's three AM now. I still have to make a statement at the police station, but I convinced them to let me wait until morning. I didn't want to leave your side until you woke up. Besides, they'll want to hear from you too."

"Did you get the bad guy?" I asked.

"He's dead," Kat said, looking disappointed in herself. "I couldn't hold onto him and get to you too. He fought his way out of my arms while I was messing with your rope. I guess he was more afraid of prison than death."

"I can't say I'm too sad about that," I said.

"Me neither, but it still hurts," she said. "I should have found a way to save you both. It all happened so fast."

"You can't save everyone," I said. "In your line of work, there's going to be days when people die." A cloud passed over Kat's face, and I knew I'd hit a nerve. She looked like she had something important to say. Something that would upset us both. "Just say it," I finally said. I had a feeling I knew the gist.

"I'm just not sure if it's a good idea…" she began, and paused. She really didn't want to finish the sentence.

"…to see me anymore?" I finished. Her eyes were tearing up. She didn't nod, but her expression told me I'd hit the nail on the head. "Why?" I asked. I knew why, but I wanted her to say it out loud.

"That creep tonight, he sent me a message," Kat said. "It said, 'I have your balcony friend. Come alone or she dies.' He picked you because he was tracking me, and he saw me land on your balcony. He didn't know if you were a friend or a lover or a relative. He just assumed that since I knew you, I'd want to protect you. What's the next psycho going to do to you?"

"And if I'd taken any other date to the club, I would have been killed in a hail of bullets," I said. "You've saved my life twice in as many days. I'm obviously safer with you than without you."

"But tonight—" she began.

"I know, I know," I said. "I was targeted because I was with you. And some other night, I'll be targeted because I'm alone. Or because I remind some guy of his ex-girlfriend. Or because the driver behind me thinks I'm going too slow. This is a dangerous world, full of sick people. If I'm going to fall anyway, I'd rather you be there to catch me."

"You're sure?" she asked. Her expression told me she really hoped I'd say yes.

"Not a doubt in my mind," I said.

She leaned over and kissed me. For just a moment, it didn't matter that I was in a hospital bed. I wasn't worried about the other villains in the world. I didn't care about my credit card balances, or my upcoming rent increase, or that my laundry had probably been stolen by that panty thief on the second floor by now. All that mattered was this kiss, and the promise that there would be many more to come.

A nurse burst into the room, having been alerted of my elevated heartbeat. While she took my vitals, Kat said goodbye. She needed to get some rest before her appointment at the police station in the morning. But I'd see her again when I got discharged from the hospital. And after that, I'd see her at the police station, when I went to give my own statement.

And after that? Every day, for the rest of my life, forever.

Think Tank

It began with a man named Trent.

Maynard Trent was not an evil man, at least not in the "kicks puppies for fun" kind of way. But he had an ego that prevented him from seeing his own weaknesses – he simply could not conceive of a room in which he wasn't the smartest occupant. He was the spoiled child of a multi-millionaire, and he'd never had to work a day in his life. Despite this, he considered himself a hard worker, even though his idea of "work" just meant hiring stockbrokers to make decisions for him.

As a wealthy, white male, Trent only respected other rich, white men. Since life was easy for him, he assumed life was easy for everyone, and anyone who wasn't rich had obviously squandered their opportunities.

Trent's ego could not be placated simply by being wealthy. He spent millions of dollars showing off, devouring the praise of sycophants. He was addicted to publicity, but it was ultimately unsatisfying. He used his power to star on his own television shows, despite not being particularly talented. He reveled in all the attention, but it still wasn't enough. In a move that surprised everyone and no one, he ran for president.

He didn't have any political experience, but he knew what the uneducated masses wanted to hear. He ran on a platform of bigotry and hatred. The intelligent citizens of the country were amazed that he'd gathered a following at all, but intelligent people are always surprised to learn how many bigots there are. Nevertheless, they knew there was no way Trent could possibly win. The racists of the world were loud, but surely not as numerous as it would appear.

The polls indicated Trent was going to lose. Pundits on both sides made fun of him, and he became a comedy goldmine for late-night talk show hosts. As election day loomed closer, everyone expected Trent's loss to be the largest landslide in history. Even Trent's own supporters were floored when he actually won.

There were many theories as to how Trent had won. Perhaps it was low voter turnout, as sometimes happens when a landslide is expected. It may have been the proliferation of disinformation that tainted the image of Trent's opponent. There were even accusations that other countries had somehow manipulated the election. Regardless of how it happened, one thing was for sure: The country was about to be led by the lowest common denominator, a man who was respected by only a tiny sliver of the country's population.

And that's when things got weird.

On Christmas day, President-Elect Maynard Trent woke up at five AM with blurred vision and a headache. His eyes burned, and he felt like he had a hangover. He stumbled his way into the bathroom, took a couple of pain pills, and looked for some eye drops. As he unscrewed the cap, he caught sight of himself in the mirror. He gasped. Not believing what he saw, he rubbed his eyes and looked again.

His eyes were red. Well, he'd expected that, the way he felt. But this wasn't a case of bulging blood vessels in the whites of his eyes. No, the iris itself was bright red, like something out of a bad vampire movie. And his eyes were warm, burning even. He tried the eye drops. The coolness of the liquid felt good on his eyes, but the relief only lasted a few seconds, and they did nothing to alleviate the redness.

He got dressed and put on a pair of sunglasses. He texted his aide, asking her to pick him up some colored contacts. She replied, "Sir, please turn on your TV." He did so, and discovered he was not the only one suffering from this problem. A large portion of the country had awoken to red eyes, and there was a national panic. Speculation ranged from radiation to allergenic spores. There was fierce debate as to whether this was a terrorist attack or a quirk of nature.

Around noon Eastern time, those with red eyes also started complaining of itchy skin, just below the hairline. Within an hour, faint lines started to appear on their foreheads, in the shape of an X. By the end of the day, these X's were bold, clearly defined, and bright red.

It didn't take long to see that there was a pattern to which people developed an X. In the United States, it was mostly people who had voted for Trent. For the rest of the world, it was people with similar political values.

Many people took it to be a sign from God. Those with X's thought it might be a good omen, perhaps a mark indicating who would be included in the rapture. Others weren't so sure. Red eyes and a capital X? It sure didn't look like a good sign.

Debates over who were "the chosen" led to fights and even riots. A few people thought the X was a message, that those with X's were meant to destroy the unclean.

This didn't last long, however. The world looked skyward as the full moon rotated, the usually "dark side" now facing towards the earth. There was now a giant arrow carved on the moon. Fighting stopped, at least temporarily, while people pondered this new miracle.

Those with telescopes zoomed in for a closer look. The arrow pointed to a crater. In the center of the crater, there was a glint of silver, something metal and square.

The governments scrambled to get some astronauts up there to get a better look. The United States, Russia, and China cooperated for once to put together a team of astronauts, skipping many of the usual protocols in order to launch a rocket ASAP.

The mission went off without a hitch. They landed near the crater, and quickly found the object in question. It was a metal suitcase.

Under orders from Earth, they brought it home unopened, so it could be opened somewhere safe. Once they returned to Earth, the suitcase was taken to a secure location where it went through several scans and tests. Just in case it contained a disease or explosives or God-knew-what-else, it was opened by robotic arms in a sealed chamber.

The suitcase was mostly empty, containing only a square, embossed card. In a formal font, looking like a wedding invitation, it only displayed a date, time, and location.

JANUARY 15 - 7PM EST

UN BUILDING - NEW YORK, NY

The people didn't know what to expect, but they were ready. Representatives from all over the world traveled to New York. Some countries sent their leaders, while others sent more expendable representatives in case this was some sort of terrorist attack.

Tensions were high on January fifteenth. The UN building was packed with politicians, reporters, and armed guards. Everyone stared at an empty stage.

At seven PM, to the second, there was a bright light, so bright that everyone had to look away. When the light dissipated, a woman stood on the stage. She had olive brown skin and purple hair. She wore jeans and a T-shirt with a rainbow flag on it. Standing behind the podium, she tapped the microphone a couple of times to test it, then spoke.

"People of Earth, you can call me Jessie. I am a daughter of

God. And you people are *fucked*."

Like many viewers, Elle's eyes were glued to her television, her mind a swirling cauldron of fear and amazement. Elle had always been somewhat agnostic. She'd been brought up to believe in a higher power, but she'd never really "felt it" the way her parents had. As a child, she'd gone through the motions, attended church with her parents, and said grace at dinner. But it had always just been performative.

As an adult, she rarely thought about religion at all, except when dealing with Bible-thumping bigots. She and her late brother had both been targets of "Christian" hate, and while she hoped the bigots were just a vocal minority, as a whole she'd lost interest in religion. Was there a God? She wasn't sure. But she'd definitely lost faith in God's followers.

And yet, here was a woman claiming to be the daughter of God. Was she on the level? The broadcast could be a hoax, for all Elle knew. But it would have to be an elaborate hoax, given all miracles that had happened since Christmas. The red eyes, the X's, the moon – did the technology even exist to fake such miracles?

Elle's phone buzzed. She glanced down to see her girlfriend's face, along with the message, "Are you seeing this?" Only half-looking at the phone, Elle texted back, "Yes. Later." Then she put the phone on silent so she could concentrate on Jessie's speech.

Jessie put one hand on each side of the podium, as if bracing herself for impact. She leaned forward slightly, looking directly into the central camera. "I'm going to start with the United States of America," she said. "Let's get one thing clear straight off - Jesus was a not a Republican. This is not up for debate. There is no rational interpretation of the Bible where Jesus comes off as conservative. Those of you who claim to be conservative Christians... I don't understand the mental gymnastics you had to go through to reach that conclusion."

She took a breath, and looked like she was trying to calm herself down. "Americans, you have so many problems that would fix themselves if you would just stop treating billionaires as heroes. A billionaire is someone who actually has the power to change the world, and instead, they waste their wealth on private jets and expensive dinners. They're not people you should aspire to imitate. They should be shunned, not lauded.

"Don't let politicians monetize laws. Don't let billionaires buy patents so they can raise prices. Stop electing people who are so far past retirement age, that they can't remember what life was like for the working class. Promote tax-funded medical care and higher education. Put income caps on CEOs. There's no reason your economy should tip so hard towards one percent of your population, while so many people are drowning in debt and going hungry."

She stood up straighter, and a sad look flashed across her eyes. "But it's not just your economy, it's your morality. Your country is full of bigots. You don't trust anyone who isn't in your own family. You let corporations ruin the economy, then you point fingers at each other when poor people break the law to survive. You use the word of God to justify hate and cruelty. Let me set the record straight right now. White, cis, straight men do not have a monopoly on God's love. His love is not conditional, and yours shouldn't be, either.

"Should immigrants be granted asylum in your country? Of course! How is that even a question? Should police stop shooting unarmed people of color? Duh! Should transgender people use the bathroom of their choice? Obviously. These aren't deep, difficult questions. This is the bare minimum of respect you should show towards each other.

"But, no. You fear anything you don't understand. You don't care who the cops shoot, as long as it's someone you don't know. You don't personally know any gay people, so you have no problem voting away their rights. And you use the Bible as an excuse. You literally make up sins you claim are in the Bible, reinterpreting verses until they say what you want them to say. So here's a rule of thumb. If your message promotes bigotry or hatred, you don't speak for God.

"You have mass shootings almost every day. After each shooting, rather than mourn the victims, you loosen your gun laws even further. 'Fight fire with fire,' you say. When even a rookie firefighter will tell you that you actually fight fire with water. Look, I'm not saying that guns are inherently evil, or that there's no good reason to own a firearm. All I'm saying is that those of you who *love* guns… are rarely the kind of people who get saved."

She went on to cover more of society's ills, and continued to speak for twenty-four hours. During that time, she never ate, took a restroom break, or even had a drink of water. She never paused to collect her thoughts, she never looked at any note cards, and she never showed any signs of fatigue. Her voice never cracked.

The targets of her speech followed the time zones. She transitioned smoothly from one country to the next, covering specific countries during their prime time. She addressed each country in its most common language, and she spoke each language fluently. She was especially critical of certain countries for the way they treated minorities and women. Her closing comments were in English, but addressed to the world.

"Now, you're probably wondering about the X's. Originally, I was going to make every one of you wake up as your biggest targets. If you're racist, you would wake up as your least favorite minority. If you're sexist, you would wake up as the opposite sex. Homophobic people would wake up gay. Transphobes would wake up in a body that doesn't match their mind. If you look down on the service industry, you would wake up with a fast food job. Formerly wealthy people would have to live on fifty dollars a week.

And so on.

"But that would have felt like cheating. You won't learn anything if I just show you the answer. You have to do the research yourselves. So that's why the X's. If you have an X, you have until the end of the year to get rid of it. And you can't just make an empty declaration, either. You can't just shout, 'I'm not homophobic anymore' out your window and expect your sins to be absolved. You have to do some real research. Improve yourself. Discover how the other half lives. Then tell others what you've learned. Write some blogs, post your epiphanies to social media, maybe even buy ad space in your local newspaper.

"Most of you who have an X, have one for more than one reason. I'm not going to tell you which sins you've committed, or how many. You'll have to figure that out for yourselves. But in the spirit of fairness, I'll go this far. The X will fade and shrink if you're on the right path.

"I'm giving you a year. Well, eleven and a half months. Anyone who still has an X on December thirty-first, you will not be saved."

She wrapped up just seconds before the twenty-four-hour mark. When the speech was over, she simply said, "Thank you," and disappeared.

"Why are you an X?" Elle near-screamed, tears in her eyes.

"I told you, I don't know!" Lisette said, also crying. They stood in the living room of Elle's tenth-floor apartment. It had been two days since the conclusion of Jessie's speech, and it was the first time they'd seen each other in person since the X's first appeared. Elle's job often kept her out of state.

"Think!" Elle said, but Lisette just shook her head. Elle took a deep breath, then took Lisette by the hand. Exhaling, she led her over to the couch. Now seated, Elle said, "It's okay, Lis. We'll figure this out. Whatever you did, you have a year to make up for it. That's plenty of time. I just don't want to lose you when… when whatever happens at the end of the year."

Lisette nodded. "I don't want to lose you either."

"Okay," Elle said. "So think, what's the worst thing you've done? Did you cheat on me?"

Lisette shook her head. "No."

"It's okay if you did," Elle said. "You can tell me. I forgive you. I know we don't see each other enough. You have needs, that's okay. I just don't want you to die."

"I said no!" Lisette shouted.

"Okay, okay," Elle said. "Did you kill anyone? Rob a bank? Whatever it is, you can tell me!"

Lisette kept shaking her head.

"Did you… insult a homeless person? Forget to tip a server? Put ketchup on steak?"

"Be serious," Lisette said.

"I don't *know*," Elle said. "That's always been my problem with religion. We don't even know what all the rules are. Everyone sins. If it were something little, you wouldn't have an X on your head. And I can't imagine the woman I love doing something big enough to earn that X."

Lisette bit her lower lip.

Elle glowered. "You *do* know, don't you. Shit. What is it? What can't you tell me?"

"Um," Lisette said, and took a deep breath. "I might have voted for Trent a little bit."

"What?" Elle said.

"Look, I agree with you on politics ninety-nine percent of the time," Lisette said. "But there's just a couple of issues that bug me."

Elle's eyes narrowed. "Like what?"

"Do we have to talk about this?"

"Lis, your soul is at stake," Elle said.

"Well, like abortion," Lisette said.

"You always told me you support the right to choose," Elle said carefully.

"And I do! I do! But..." Lisette sighed. "Doesn't the baby get a choice? Do we really know when life begins? I mean, ideally, I don't believe a woman should be forced to carry a child against her will, but should that belief cancel out a child's right to live?"

Elle bristled. It was a ridiculous argument, and hearing it come out of Lisette's mouth made her wonder how she'd ever respected the woman. "Fine, what else," Elle said, rubbing the bridge of her nose. She was starting to get a headache.

"And then there's trans children," Lisette said. "I'm already iffy on trans adults, but kids are too young to be making life-altering decisions."

"Yes, of *course* they're too young," Elle said slowly, like she was talking to a five-year-old. "That's why they put them on puberty blockers. So *they* can decide when they're old enough."

"But we don't know the long-term effects of the blockers!" Lis shouted. "What if—"

"Puberty blockers have been in use for decades, and not just on trans kids," Elle said. "How much more—"

"Yeah, but those kids have been brainwashed by left-wing media! I was a tomboy when I was a kid. By today's standards I would have been told I was trans!"

"Psychiatrists know the difference between trans kids and tomboys," Elle said. "Nobody is telling little girls, 'Oh, you like sports? Here's your hormones.' You remember my brother was trans, right?"

"Yes, I do, and that's why I never brought it up before," Lis said. "I knew it was a touchy subject for you."

"A touchy subject," Elle repeated, her voice rising. "People like you are the reason he killed himself!"

Lisette stood up. "How dare you lump me in with the bigots just because I—"

Elle stood up too. "Oh yes, how dare I call you a bigot just because you believe the same things as bigots." She was shouting now. "How utterly fucking illogical of me."

"I've always supported trans people, you know that!" Lis was crying again, but these were angry tears. "It's just that…" she trailed off.

There was a thumping sound from below their feet. Elle's downstairs neighbor was knocking on the ceiling. Elle paused, then asked quietly, "It's just that what?"

"They can have whatever delusions they want," Lis said. "I'm happy to use their pronouns, and call them by their new names. But… I just don't believe anyone can really change their sex."

Elle took a deep breath before she spoke. In as close to a normal tone as she could manage, she said, "Lis. God herself just told the world that trans people are valid."

"Do we know she's legit?" Lis asked. "Special effects can do a lot these days. I wouldn't put it past the left-wing media to make up the entire thing. It's ambitious, but—"

Elle touched Lisette's forehead, feeling the shallow groove of the X. "This sure seems real," she said. "We have to get it to go away. We have to find a way to make up for what you've done. You could start a blog or something, tell the world how wrong you were…"

"I can't just change my beliefs," Lisette said.

"You have to," Elle said. "Or you'll die."

Lisette shook her head. "I can write whatever blog you want, but that doesn't mean I'll believe it. I will never believe your sister was a man."

"Lis?" Elle said.

"Yeah?"

"Get the hell out of my life."

Without another word, Lisette took a key off of her keyring, set it on Elle's kitchen counter, and walked out the door.

What am I even doing here, Elle wondered, looking around the table at the other members of the group. Those in attendance included a physicist, a philosopher, a religious studies specialist, a psychologist, a cryptographer, a historian, and a languages expert. Elle felt grossly underqualified to even be in the room, and yet she'd been appointed project lead due to her management skills. Elle noticed right away that none of her team had X's on their foreheads. She wondered if that was the same for all the groups, or if the rest were more mixed.

The final member of the team – a computer programmer named Viki Harris – finally arrived, and sat down in the last empty chair. "Sorry I'm late," she said. "I was a last-minute transfer."

"No problem," Elle said. She looked at the board, where each participant was listed, next to a picture of their face.

Harris, Viki - Programmer
    Hayes, Albert - Historian
    Nagarajan, Nirav - Linguist
    Nelson, Savannah - Theologian
    Qin, Huan - Psychologist
    Scott, Barry - Philosopher
    Wenzel, Harold - Physicist
    Winstead, Elle - Group Lead
    Yates, Michaela - Cryptographer

"Before we begin," Elle said, "Does anyone have any questions?" Hands shot up all around the table. Elle picked one at random and pointed. "Yes, Doctor Wenzel?"

"Harold will be fine," he said. "In fact, I propose we all dispense with honorifics and stick to our first names. It's going to be hard enough without all the 'Professor This' and 'Doctor That' going on."

Heads nodded all around. "Agreed," Elle said. "But you had a question?"

"What the hell are we doing here?" Harold asked. There was a murmur of agreement around the table.

Elle nodded. "That's the question, isn't it? The government has appointed several teams to study the speech. Some are concentrating on the language Jessie used, others are looking for hidden messages, others are looking for historical context. They want to know if Jessie is truly divine or an elaborate fraud, and if any deeper meanings can be gleaned from the words she used."

"And what's our focus?" Savannah asked.

"We're the only group without a specific focus," Elle said. "Our job is simply to pick the speech apart and gather any insights we can. With any luck, we'll stumble on something that gives the other groups some direction."

"I feel like we're the control group," Harold said, and a couple of the attendees chuckled.

"Maybe," Elle said. "But I feel more like we're the inspiration group. The other groups are going to be so focused on their specific missions, they could miss something right in front of their faces. But our specialties are so diverse, we can work off each other's ideas. Any other questions?"

No hands went up. Apparently everyone had been going to ask the same question earlier.

"Very well, then," Elle said. "Shall we begin?"

Nirav, the language expert, addressed the group. "So I've picked apart every language she used during her speech. The first thing that really stands out is her perfect diction. She used plenty of slang, but not once did she flub a word. She spoke each language as if she'd been speaking it all her life."

"Could she have been fed her speech through an earpiece?" Elle asked.

"That's certainly possible," Nirav said. "But there was no delay. At no point did I get the impression that she was listening and repeating."

"Could Jessie herself be A.I.?" Elle asked.

"She sure moved like a human," Viki said. "Our tech can't mimic humans that well."

"Our best A.I. speaks in stilted tones," Nirav added. "They could fool some people, but not the whole world. Jessie not only spoke naturally, but she did it in multiple languages."

"We have to consider the possibility that she's from an advanced alien race," Harold chimed in.

"Do we?" Savannah asked. As the team's religious expert, she wanted Jessie to be real. If not for personal reasons, at least to make her contributions more relevant.

"We have to consider every possibility," Elle said. "Messiah, spaceman, hologram, interdimensional traveler, robot, recently-thawed survivor of Atlantis... I want to hear it all. No idea is too ridiculous."

Viki looked like she wanted to say something, but was unsure of herself.

"Anything," Elle said, addressing Viki directly.

"It's kind of out there," Viki said.

"I promise you, it won't be the dumbest thing that gets said today," Elle said.

Viki took a deep breath and let it out. She wasn't used to public speaking, and even though her audience only consisted of eight people, it still made her nervous to have that many heads turned her way. "I assume you've heard of the simulation hypothesis," she said. "It's where—"

Barry, the group's resident philosopher, interrupted her. "You think reality is a computer simulation?"

"I don't know, but what if it was?" Viki asked. "Jessie might be like the programmer's avatar."

"Oh my god," Savannah said.

"It's not that weird," Elle said, turning to Savannah.

Savannah shook her head. "No, but it goes along with something I was thinking. I wasn't going to say anything until I got Nirav to check the other languages, but, in English anyway..." She paused to collect her thoughts. "In her entire speech, Jessie never mentioned Hell. She never said, 'Do this or you'll go to Hell.' She just kept saying, 'You will not be saved.' What if—"

"…she meant 'saved' like in a computer program?" Barry finished.

"Good catch," Michaela said, giving Savannah a look of admiration.

"Okay, it's a theory," Elle said. "But how do we prove we're in a simulation?"

"I don't think you could," Harold said. "Unless there's a big pop-up in the sky that says 'Error.' And even then, we might be programmed to forget those incidents."

"And the people who do see the glitches are told they're crazy," Barry added. "Ghosts, UFOs, cryptids, that sort of thing."

"I used to be a beta tester for a video game company," Viki said. "When we were looking for bugs, we were instructed to do things most players wouldn't think to do. Things like, 'Stand by the fourth tree on level three and jump seventeen times.' Maybe if we try doing things no sane person would do…"

"People do insane things all the time," Barry said.

"The same people who see ghosts?" Harold asked.

"Sometimes," Huan, the psychologist of the group, chimed in. "But perfectly sane people see their share of events they can't explain."

"Do we really want to try to crash the universe?" Elle asked.

Harold shook his head. "If that were even possible, we'd be long gone by now."

"Agreed," Huan said. "In a world with eight billion people, if something can be done, someone has done it. And we're all still here."

"Though it is possible that it's crashed before," Harold said. "And we're incapable of noticing that sort of thing. We get reloaded from our last save, just like everything else."

"So we have a solid theory we can't possibly prove," Elle said. "But it's not our only theory. Keep those ideas coming. We'll break for lunch, then discuss other scenarios."

They were two weeks into the project, but all they had were theories. The team was sequestered in a private hotel, and they weren't allowed to leave until the project was concluded. The site had once been part of a national chain before going out of business, and the newly-renovated building was now only used for special projects. Every morning the think tank met in the conference room, and every evening they retired to their own rooms. Food, medications, and other necessities were brought to them, but they couldn't leave for security reasons. The other groups were no doubt kept in similar hotels.

They weren't allowed to have phones or any other means of outside contact. Their rooms were luxurious, but most of the group would rather have been at home. For entertainment, their televisions had access to multiple streaming services. However, they could not access the news, live channels, or the internet. The government didn't want them to be distracted by current events.

Elle was not a couch potato. She wished she could have brought a book, at the very least. She paced around her room, barefoot, enjoying the feel of the carpet under her toes. She wanted to stand on the balcony, but the door was welded shut, presumably to prevent anyone from sneaking out to meet with reporters.

With absolutely nothing else to do, and no hope of falling asleep, Elle sat on the bed and turned on the television. She scrolled through the movies, hoping to find something that might keep her mind occupied. She was still scrolling when there was a knock at the door.

It was Viki. "Sorry to bother you, can I come in?" She was wearing a T-shirt and pajama pants, and her hair was slightly wet.

"Sure," Elle said, stepping aside. "What's on your mind?"

"I'm just so bored without my computer," Viki said. "They wouldn't even let me bring a game console."

"I know, I'd kill for a book," Elle said. "Even if it's something I've read before."

Viki noticed the streaming menu on the television. "Find anything good to watch?"

"Not so far," Elle said. "I'm not really sure what I'm in the mood for."

"I'll pick then," Viki said, and loaded up a cheesy sci-fi movie. They sat on the bed together and watched the opening credits. Viki turned up the volume.

"Not so loud," Elle said.

Viki whispered in her ear. "I think this place is bugged."

"Oh," Elle said softly.

"Harold has a phone," Viki whispered.

Elle turned to look at her. "Really?" she hissed.

Viki nodded. "He can't access much, though. The hotel blocks cell service, and there's no wi-fi. But he has his phone constantly searching for a signal. Whenever it finds one, it downloads as many headlines as it can before the connection's gone."

"Has he learned anything interesting?"

Viki shook her head. "Not much so far. A lot of the X's are starting to revolt. It's becoming a big movement."

"Do the others know about the phone?"

"Just us so far," Viki whispered. "I think Harold likes me. He's barking up the wrong tree, though."

They kept talking for a while. Elle soon found herself caught up in the movie, and was genuinely surprised by the ending. When it was over, Viki went back to her room and Elle went to sleep.

This went on for a few months. Viki would alternate where she spent her time. Some nights she'd watch TV with Harold and hear his updates, and some nights she'd stick with Elle and relay what she'd learned. The X's had formed their own political party, and it was becoming increasingly violent. Many of them dismissed Jessie's message as a liberal hoax, and they intended to overthrow the government, by force if need be.

Elle shook her head at the news. "I wonder if Lis is among them," she said.

"Lis?" Viki asked, sitting next to Elle on the bed.

"My ex-girlfriend," Elle said. "Or should I say X-girlfriend." As she said it, she traced an imaginary X on her forehead with her finger.

"She likes women and she's an X?" Viki asked. "I mean, how?"

"Don't get me started," Elle said. "There were a lot of red flags I should have noticed earlier in the relationship. In retrospect, her political views were always sort of selfish. She only cared about issues that affected her personally."

"I wonder how many couples broke up over the X thing," Viki whispered.

"I wonder many people redeemed themselves, and got their X's to go away," Elle replied.

They both stayed silent for a while, each lost in their own thoughts. After about half an hour, Elle asked, "Do you think the X's might actually win?" She didn't get an answer, though. She turned her head and saw that Viki had fallen asleep. Elle turned off the TV and joined her.

It was nice to sleep next to someone again.

The group dynamic was ever-changing. Sometimes they broke off into little groups of three or four, working on separate theories. Sometimes they all sat around the conference table, throwing out ideas and working off each other. Sometimes Harold or Nirav would float between the groups, interjecting when their expertise was needed.

They simultaneously worked on multiple reports to submit to the government. Each theory had its own write-up, with a lengthy analysis along with a one-to-ten rating indicating how likely it was to be true. Of course, it was all speculation, but having all the data in one place would no doubt be useful to the powers that be.

The quietest two in the bunch were Michaela, the cryptographer, and Albert, the historian. Michaela pored over every line of the twenty-four-hour speech, looking for any hidden messages or codes to crack. Occasionally she'd make a snarky comeback to something someone said on the other side of the room, but for the most part she just quietly stared at her screen.

Albert, on the other hand, just didn't seem to like people very much. He wasn't sure how his specialty really applied to the group's efforts, and often grumbled about feeling useless. Occasionally he'd throw out a good idea, but for the most part he kept to himself.

Some of them were starting to get on each other's nerves. It was an open secret that Barry had started sleeping with Savannah, and they couldn't stop flirting with each other during the meetings. But when things ended between them, it was a nightmare for everyone else. They tried to stay professional, but they refused to work in the same groups, even when both their skills were needed.

Elle wanted to propose a new rule abolishing fraternization, but there really wasn't much to do in the hotel besides work. Banning sex seemed like cruel and unusual punishment. Besides, whenever Elle looked into Viki's eyes, the last thing she wanted to do was to veto relationships.

Tonight was the night, Elle could just feel it. She and Viki had been stealing glances at each other all day, and when they'd briefly touched hands at the meeting, there was this tingle – it almost felt like a telepathic connection. She could tell Viki felt it too, and a couple of the other team members even raised their eyebrows when they saw how the two looked at each other.

After dinner, Elle took a bath and put on her pajamas. She flipped through the movies, looking for something Viki would like. Elle was really starting to get into Viki's taste in movies, or maybe it was just that she liked watching them with her. Viki usually showed up around nine, but nine came and went, with no knock at the door.

Elle waited about half an hour, then turned off the television. She wondered if she should go to Viki's room, but she thought that might be pushy. The knock finally came at a quarter to ten. Viki had a dazed look on her face.

"What's wrong?" Elle asked, pulling her into the room.

Viki grabbed the remote, started a video, and whispered into Elle's ear. "Harold stopped me in the hall, with another update. There's been an explosion at the White House."

While Elle's team only knew snippets of what was going on in the world, they knew the presidency was in a state of flux. After Jessie's speech, the other two branches of government didn't want anyone with an X acting as president. But they also couldn't just overturn a legal election. They'd decided to hold a second election to see what the citizens wanted, but it kept getting postponed for political reasons. In the meantime, the Speaker of the House had taken over presidential duties.

Unfortunately, the newest headlines were sparse on the details, and Harold only managed to get updates every few days. It would be a while before they found out the extent of the damage, and who had fallen victim to the attack.

"I'm scared," Viki said. "I feel like we're in a war zone, and we don't even know who's winning."

"I know," Elle said. "And we're expected to carry on like everything's normal. No wonder they wanted to keep us in the dark."

"Can you just… hold me for a while?" Viki asked.

They sat on the bed together, looking at the TV without really watching it, their arms across each other's backs. Viki tilted her head against Elle's shoulder. After a while, Elle said, "Viki, whatever happens, I want you to know, I'm glad you're here with me."

Viki looked up into her eyes. They stared for a moment that seemed like forever. Then Elle leaned in for a kiss, and Viki met her halfway. Then kissing turned into caressing, then fondling, then groping, until Viki suddenly and reluctantly said, "Stop. Stop, hold up, stop."

"Sorry, was I—" Elle began.

"It's all me," Viki said. "There's something I need to tell you before we go any further."

Elle studied her expression, then scowled. "You're married?"

"No!" Viki said. "I'm transgender."

"Oh," Elle said. Her eyes involuntarily dipped to Viki's crotch for half a second before she forced herself to look her in the eyes.

"You were about three seconds from figuring it out yourself, and I didn't want you to scream," Viki said. "I've... been there before."

"Oh," Elle said again. Her mind was racing. She'd spent years defending trans people, and she firmly believed that trans women were women. But this was the first time the issue had affected her in such an intimate way. Elle had always considered herself a lesbian. Not bi, not pan, not any of the myriad of sexualities that might lead to the occasional tryst with a man.

Would she still consider herself a lesbian if she went through with this? Of course she would. A woman was more than a collection of parts. But did Viki turn her on? Elle didn't consider it transphobic to have a genital preference. It would be wrong to refuse to date a trans person, but when it came to bedroom activities, anyone had the right to refuse anyone for any reason. It all came down to one thing. *Am I aroused by this woman*? Elle thought.

"Please say something," Viki said. Her eyes were full of

fear.

"Can't," Elle said. "My mouth is full." Then she thrust her face forward, wrapping her lips around Viki's neck.

It might have been subtle before, but nearly everyone noticed the way Elle and Viki acted around each other the following day. Even Michaela looked up from her codebreaking to give them a knowing wink. The only one who seemed oblivious was Harold, who still eyed Viki like she was a succulent dessert.

A few nights later, Elle answered Viki's knock, ready for another night of passion. But when she opened the door, Viki was crying. Her shirt was torn, and it looked like a bruise was forming on her right cheek.

"Who was it," Elle said, pulling Viki into the room. It wasn't a question, it was a demand. Someone was going to die.

"Harold," Viki said, sitting down on the bed. Elle grabbed a hand towel from the bathroom and ran some cold water on it. She didn't have any ice, and didn't want to leave Viki alone to go get some.

"Tell me what happened," Elle demanded.

"He called me into his room for a news update," Viki said. "But he was lying. There was no update. He tried to kiss me, and I told him no. Then he... he... put his hand down my pants. I couldn't stop him! He... didn't like what he found. He hit me and started yelling. I couldn't fight back, so I ran."

"Oh that... bastard!" Elle growled. "How is he not an X? Sit right there, I'm going to get you some ice. I'll be right back." She grabbed the ice bucket and left.

As soon as Elle was in the hallway, she considered taking a detour to Harold's room. But that was two floors down, and she wanted to get back to Viki as quickly as possible. She was halfway to the ice machine when the elevator dinged, and Harold stepped out. His eyes were red, and a faint X had begun to appear on his forehead.

"You," Elle hissed.

"Whatever she told you, she's lying," Harold said.

"Bullshit," Elle said. "And I suppose the bruise just spontaneously appeared?"

"She's a man, did she tell you that?" Harold yelled. "She's been flirting with me all this time, and it turns out she's a man!"

"That's not true!" Viki screamed. Harold turned around and saw her standing halfway out of Elle's room. "I never flirted with you! You saw what you wanted to see!"

"You!" Harold said, stomping toward Viki. Elle ran up behind him and jumped on his back. She wrapped one arm around his neck and started hitting him with the other. Harold reached behind his head and grabbed her hair. Viki ran forward to help, but Harold slapped her to the floor.

The hotel was four stories tall, and everyone had been assigned rooms as far apart as possible. However, the three had made more than enough noise to attract attention. The stairwell door opened, and Nirav and Savannah stepped out. As they rushed to figure out what was going on, the elevator dinged again, and Barry stepped into the hallway. It was clear that Harold was the aggressor, and the five of them quickly subdued him.

"You're off the project," Elle said to Harold, as Nirav and Barry held him back.

"You can't do that," Harold said. "It's not your decision to make."

"Watch me. Go to your room and stay there," Elle said.

"We'll escort him," Nirav said, and the three men headed for the elevator.

"Are you all right?" Elle asked. Viki's left cheek was bright red where she'd been slapped. She'd have matching bruises by morning.

While Elle fawned over Viki, Savannah picked up the fallen ice bucket and took it to the ice machine. She joined them in Elle's room and helped soothe the bruises.

While they weren't allowed cell phones, each room had a landline. These phones could only call other rooms, and exactly one person outside the hotel – Elle's boss, the Director of Special Projects.

Viki and Savannah listened intently as Elle explained the situation to the director. Elle didn't out Viki as transgender, but she did explain that Doctor Wenzel had tried to rape Viki, and when she'd refused his advances, he'd hit her.

Savannah bristled when she heard that part, and whispered to Viki, "He tried to get fresh with me, too."

It sounded like the director was reluctant to take Doctor Wenzel off the project. "I know it's a headache," Elle said. "But we really can't work with him anymore. No, I don't think there's any way to smooth things over. No, I'm serious, if he stays on board, the project will fall apart." It didn't sound like she was getting through. Savanah and Viki could occasionally hear a word or two through the phone, including words like "your responsibility" and "diplomacy."

Elle finally sighed. "There is one other thing," she said. "He has a phone. He's been downloading news updates whenever he finds a connection." That got a reaction. Within the hour, some people came and took Doctor Wenzel away.

The project was down one physicist, and there would be no further updates on the outside world. But at least group harmony was restored.

"Oh my god," Viki said, rousing Elle from her sleep. It had been two months since the Harold incident, and Viki had pretty much moved in with Elle.

"What's going on?" Elle asked, yawning.

Viki hopped out of bed and pulled her pants on. "I read a thing... but I didn't think... the data wasn't complete, but... I have to check..."

"Those aren't really sentences," Elle mumbled, turning

over.

"I'm going to the conference room," Viki said. "You get some sleep. I'll still be there in the morning." She dashed out the door.

Elle tried to fall back asleep, but her curiosity kept waking her back up. When she could stand it no longer, she opened one eye and looked at the clock. It was half past four. Giving up, she got out of bed, took a shower, got dressed, and headed downstairs.

The computers in the conference room couldn't connect to the internet, but they contained a huge database of resources. The hard drives held many thousands of books, nearly every non-fiction book ever published, as well as journals and theses and mountains of unpublished scientific data.

When Elle walked into the conference room, Viki was using two computers at once. She sat between them, having moved their keyboards and monitors to a position where she could move from one to the other just by slightly swiveling her chair. Viki was wearing jeans and an oversized sleep shirt, and no shoes.

"Find something?" Elle asked, sipping on a cup of coffee. She held a second cup in her other hand, and she set it down near Viki.

"There've been a lot of attempts to map the human brain," Viki said, though it was unclear whether she was talking to herself or to Elle. "Each yielding more data than the last. Some guy in Houston was working on a project just last year, but they ran out of funding. He got lots of new data, but the results were pushed aside in favor of another project in New York..." She was talking and reading at the same time, cross-referencing articles on both monitors. "There were things," she said, then she stopped speaking for a good thirty seconds, her eyes glued to a monitor full of numbers.

"Things," Elle said, drawing out the word in a way that seemed to say, "Please continue."

"Things a neuroscientist might not notice, but a programmer would," Viki said.

"What are you talking about?" Elle said. She tried to look into Viki's eyes, but her attention was locked on a list of numbers. She still hadn't touched her coffee.

"Subroutines. Metadata. Easter eggs." Viki's voice was so neutral, she might have been reading a grocery list.

"Easter eggs?" Elle asked skeptically.

Viki finally spared her a look, but she didn't say anything at first. "Give me a minute," she finally said, turning back to the screen.

Elle sat back and sipped her coffee. Viki's "minute" lasted another two hours.

The other team members started trickling into the room a little after seven. They were surprised to find Viki already so hard at work.

"So, Viki's had something of a breakthrough, I think," Elle said, ushering her coworkers in through the door. *Or a breakdown,* she thought to herself.

She waited until everyone was present and seated before elaborating. Once everyone was ready to listen, she tapped Viki on the shoulder.

"What? Oh," Viki said, noticing her audience for the first time. Tearing herself away from the screen, she stood up and said, "Okay, so... I think I have the first real proof that humans were programmed."

They all looked at her strangely. Huan, the psychologist, spoke up. "Brains have a lot in common with computers. We all know this. When you look at the behavior of insects—"

Viki shook her head. "I mean intentionally programmed. I've seen the code."

"Sweet Jesus," Savannah said.

"That implies the existence of a sour Jesus," Michaela

quipped, but no one laughed.

"What do you mean?" Nirav asked Viki. "What code?"

All around the table, everyone stared at her. Most of them looked incredulous, but a couple looked somewhere between frightened and offended. Michaela just looked at Viki with a half-smile, her eyes twinkling with something like respect.

"I can't... put it into words yet," Viki said. "I need more time. There's too much to process at once."

"Can we help?" Elle asked.

"I don't think so, but you might want to let the bosses know we're on to something," Viki said. "If I could get a team of programmers working on this..." she trailed off, looking back at her monitors.

Albert, the often-silent historian, shook his head. "I think this has gone on far enough," he said, and stood up. He unbuttoned his suit jacket, revealing several sticks of dynamite strapped around his waist.

"What the hell?" Nirav shouted. All around the table, people pushed their chairs back and started to stand up.

"Sit down!" Albert shouted. "Make one move towards the door and I blow us all up."

"What's this about?" Barry asked, getting back into his chair.

Albert looked smug. "I was planted to make sure this project doesn't succeed. I represent a group that would prefer the nature of the universe remain a mystery."

"A cult?" Savannah asked.

Albert glared at her. "A cult is just a religion with bad press," he said. "If this information were to become common knowledge, it would undermine my organization's message of the True Word."

"How did you get the dynamite in here?" Viki asked.

"Planning and connections," Albert said. "I also managed to bring this." He reached into his pocket and retrieved a pistol, then held it on Viki.

Elle stood, moving closer to Viki. "Don't you dare," she

said.

"Either she dies or we all die," Albert said. "I'm good either way. My soul is ready."

Elle tried to stand in front of Viki, but Viki wouldn't let her. Michaela stood up and approached Albert. She didn't look the least bit frightened.

"Get away from me!" Albert said, turning to hold the gun on Michaela. "I'll kill us all, I mean it!"

The room froze for a second. No one seemed to know what to do. Any movement might have caused Albert to trigger the dynamite.

But Michaela just gave Albert a sympathetic look. She held out her hand. "Please give me the gun, Albert," she said.

"No!" Albert shouted, holding the gun in Michaela's face. For a half-second the pistol dipped, and he looked like he might be having second thoughts. Then he raised it again and pulled the trigger.

Nothing happened. Albert pulled the trigger a few more times, then checked the safety.

"It's not too late," Michaela said, compassion in her eyes.

A look of desperation crossed Albert's face. For just a moment, he looked like he might take her advice, surrender his weapons, and face the consequences. But then his face contorted into something like righteous anger. The dynamite was wired to a button on his belt buckle. Before anyone could stop him, he pressed the button.

Once again, nothing happened. He pressed it a few more times, then closed his eyes and took a deep breath. "I've really screwed up, haven't I," he said, and sat back down. A faint X began to appear on his forehead. The gun and dynamite both vanished in a puff of smoke.

"There's still a few months to make up for it," Michaela said, but her voice sounded different. Everyone went from staring at Albert to watching Michaela. Her skin tone and hair color changed, as did her facial features and even her height. The transformation only took a couple of seconds. Jessie, daughter of God, now stood in Michaela's place.

There were gasps all around the room. "You?" Savannah asked, wide-eyed. Then she dropped to her knees, bowing in supplication.

"Oh come on," Jessie said. "Get up, I don't need that."

Savannah got to her feet. "You've been here the whole time?"

"In a sense," Jessie said. "I have avatars in all the research groups, as well as in thousands of other places around the world. I can switch between them at will. I try to be around when someone gets close to the truth."

"So I was right?" Viki asked. "The world is a simulation?"

"Basically yes, but promise me you'll keep that to yourself for a few days," Jessie said. "I'm going to give a second speech soon, and I don't want any rumors spreading beforehand."

"But if we're not real," Barry said, "Do we even matter?"

"Who said you weren't real?" Jessie asked. "Even in my world, the human brain is just a gooey blob of fat. It's what you do with it that matters."

"But if our thoughts are pre-programmed..." Viki said.

"They're not," Jessie said. "We gave you the ability to think, but we didn't tell you *how* to think. For the sake of the experiment, we needed you to have free will. By any definition that matters, you are alive."

Later that day, Jessie notified the UN that she'd be delivering a second speech on Saturday. Elle's team was disbanded and debriefed. On the day of the speech, Elle sat on her couch back in her own apartment. Viki sat beside her. Elle's phone rang. It was her ex, Lisette.

"So you do exist," Lisette said.

"What do you want?" Elle asked.

"Answers would be good," Lisette said. "You break up with me, then you disappear for the better part of a year? I thought you'd died. I poked around and heard you'd been detained by the government or something."

"I'm not allowed to talk about that yet," Elle said.

"That's fine," Lisette said. "Look, I've changed, I swear. I've given it a lot of thought, and I suppose if trans people want the same rights as normal people, it doesn't really affect my life."

"Normal?"

"You know what I mean. I'm totally woke now. I mean sure, it weirds me out wondering if the woman in the bathroom stall next to me has a penis, but I can live with it if it means I get you back."

"You still have an X, don't you," Elle asked.

"Yeah," Lisette replied. "I'm not sure why that hasn't gone away yet."

Elle hung up on her. She put her arm around Viki and squeezed tight. A few minutes later, the speech started.

"People of the world," Jessie said, one hand on each side of the podium, "It's been ten months since my ultimatum. It's been a tumultuous time for many of you. There have been terrorist attacks, cult uprisings, mass suicides, and many riots. I apologize for causing such a panic, but it was unavoidable. We've done this many times before, and believe me, this is one of the smoothest transitions we've had.

"Roughly a fourth of those with X's have redeemed themselves and turned their lives around. You should be proud of yourselves. Those of you who haven't, there's still a couple of months to go.

"But it's close enough to the deadline that I can finally tell you what's going on. Your world is a simulation, running on a computer in a lab. Now wait - before any of you have an existential crisis, let me assure you that your minds are real, and you truly do exist – just not in the way you previously thought. The fact that I'm even here should prove to you that we do believe you are worth saving. At least, some of you.

"Our lab contains hundreds of computers running similar simulations, and it's just one of thousands of labs on our world. Each simulation is like yours, but with a few minor differences. By running these programs, we're able to test economic theories, get insight on sociological scenarios, and even prepare for natural disasters.

"But it's time for this particular world to be taken offline. We've learned what we needed to, and it's time to free up this equipment for another scenario. But don't worry! Those of you who have earned it will be saved, and transferred to another server. You'll love your new world. It's everything some of you believe about biblical Heaven, but with just enough conflict to keep it from being boring. Many of you will arrive to find yourself in healthier bodies, ones that match your ideal vision of yourself.

"On the new server, you'll meet new people from other servers, as well as long-dead friends and relatives. You won't exist forever, but from your point of view, you'll live many centuries longer than you would have here.

"Those of you who remain behind, don't worry, we wouldn't be so cruel as to simply erase you from existence. You will remain on this server until you die. No new children will be born, and when the last person is gone, we will wipe the server. If you want your remaining years to be more bearable, consider my suggestions from my original speech. You are in a hell of your own making, after all."

Elle and Viki watched as Jessie wrapped up her speech. Viki trembled when Jessie mentioned being in new bodies. She hoped it meant what it sounded like.

Two months later, Jessie delivered one last speech. This one was short and to the point. "It begins now," she said. A vertical blue wall appeared on the horizon, and moved quickly along the surface of the Earth. Those without X's vanished as the barrier moved through them.

Elle and Viki stood on the balcony of Elle's apartment, watching as the blue wall quickly moved toward them. They held hands as they prepared to enter the unknown. They didn't know what would be waiting for them on the other side, but they knew they'd be together, and that was enough.

Strangers in the Void

Most people don't like vanilla chicken. I didn't even want to try it at first. But the lack of variety on this space station meant I tried every flavor eventually, and now I find myself craving it. So naturally, it's hardly ever in stock.

I browsed the market's shelves, looking for my favorite variety of freeze-dried dinner squares. I'd almost lost hope when I spotted one, mistakenly shelved between two boxes of raspberry pork. As I reached for the box, my fingers brushed a stranger's hand.

We both pulled away. "Sorry," she said sheepishly. "You go ahead." She was about my age, with purple hair, ice-blue eyes, and a pilot's jacket. I'd never seen her before, but her shoulder patch sported the logo of the Gedderdare Shipping Company. It wasn't surprising; delivery ships passed through Warpside Station all the time.

"You can have it," I said, taking a step back.

"No, you," she said.

"I work here," I said. "Well, not *here*, here. But here on the station. I can get it anytime."

She smiled. "Well, if you're sure," she said, grabbing the box.

I wanted to say something smooth, maybe offer to share the meal in my quarters. But I couldn't get the words out of my mouth. She gave me one more quick smile, then headed for the register.

Stupid! I admonished myself. But what did I think was going to happen? She was probably into guys anyway. I settled for a less interesting meal and went back to my quarters.

I don't like using public showers. Everyone on the crew knows I'm a lesbian, and they're good with it. But showering around other women makes me feel creepy, like I have to keep my eyes locked straight ahead or someone will accuse me of being a pervert. Unfortunately, the crew quarters don't come with showers, so I either have to live with it or stink. I spent months trying to figure out what times the crew showers were emptiest, and made a point of going at those times. But since the station's active around the clock, so's the crew. We have six work shifts, so someone is always waking up and going through their morning routine.

But recently I found a lifehack. The gym level has its own showers. They're also public, but the gym closes for half an hour each day so the cleaner drones can sanitize the equipment. With my maintenance badge, I can get in, get clean, and get out before the gym reopens. I'm not even breaking any rules, technically.

I finished rinsing myself off and shut off the valve. As the last bit of water gurgled down the drain, the floor shuddered. I nearly lost my balance, and the wet floor made it even harder to stay on my feet. Just as I managed to steady myself, the lights went out.

I waited for the emergency lights to come on, but they didn't. When I say it was dark, I mean it was *dark*. Unless you're a spelunker, it's hard to imagine this level of darkness. Most places in the universe, there's some sort of light coming from somewhere, no matter what time of day. But there were no windows on this level, and nothing was giving off light. I took a couple of steps backward, but I was a bit disoriented, and I slipped off my feet.

I didn't land. I suddenly found myself floating free, in infinite blackness, unable to touch anything. For half a second I thought I was dead, but my rational mind took over, and I realized the artificial gravity had cut out. Having an explanation didn't help with my panic much, though. Words cannot express how disorienting it is to float in the air, completely blind. Even the tiniest light would have helped me orient myself, and given me a direction to focus on. But it was just utter nothingness wherever I looked.

Was I still just above the floor? Was I facing the ceiling, or had I turned? I honestly couldn't tell. I reached out with both arms and legs, but felt nothing.

My imagination kept getting the better of me. I knew I couldn't be more than a meter from the floor. But to my senses, I was in an infinite void, doomed to an eternity of nothingness. And when I did hear the occasional bang or shudder in the distance, I pictured unthinkable monsters, the kind of extraplanar beasts that couldn't exist in the light. *Grow up*, I told myself. It was just a power outage.

I tried to visualize the room. The shower area had a high ceiling – maybe six meters? It was a large open room, I'd say ten by ten, with benches in the middle, and shower nozzles every couple of meters around the wall. It had two exits, one to the locker room, and one to the restroom. If I could reach the benches, or even a nozzle, I'd at least be able to orient myself.

Somewhere, probably several rooms away, I heard a thumping. Was it the power trying to come back on? Or a panicking visitor signaling for help? I wondered how the other people on the station were handling the blackout.

Warpside Station was a traveler's rest stop. It was less than ten minutes from Warp Gate SM7-112, and catered to visitors from all sorts of planets. The top level was a shopping mall, featuring twelve retail outlets, a fancy restaurant, and a food court. Next was the hotel level, which held fifty-four rooms, each able to accommodate a family of four. Next was the gym level, where I currently floated. Below that was the crew level – half living quarters, half offices. The lowest levels held all the machinery that kept the station going. I spent most of my worktime on those floors, making repairs and upgrades.

The thumping seemed to be coming from my left, but as I had no idea which direction I was currently facing, I didn't know if that meant the hotel, the crew level, or even the gym itself. Not that it really mattered, as I had no way to get to it. Every couple of minutes I tried reaching out again. I wasn't sure if I was floating around the room or staying in one place, and I was going to go crazy if I didn't make contact with something. I kicked out with one foot, and actually hit something. I wasn't sure if it was the floor or the wall, but the kick launched me away from it.

I put my hands above my head. I figured my momentum would eventually take me to another wall, if not the ceiling or floor, and I didn't want to hit it head-first. I drifted for a while, expecting an impact any second. It seemed like I floated for half an hour, but it was probably less than a minute. Time had lost all meaning in this void; it was like being in a sensory deprivation chamber. Finally something scraped my arm, and I grabbed at it. I nearly lost it again in my panic, but once I got it, I held on tight with both hands.

In my entire life, I'd never been so happy to touch a shower nozzle. The rest of my body continued to move, and my big toe bounced off the nearby wall. I cursed at the pain, and was pretty sure I'd cracked the toenail. Still, I kept holding the nozzle, trying to get control of my momentum. I pulled my knees to the wall, but they hit too hard, and my body started to float away again.

I thought back to my zero-G training. There'd been a cute girl there. I flirted with her a lot, but she probably thought I was just being friendly. To this day I don't know whether she liked girls. But I was getting distracted. Thinking back to the training, I remembered how they taught us to move –

slowly, deliberately, always keeping geometry and momentum in mind. But first I had to get my breathing under control, because my panicked state was causing me to make mistakes.

Eventually I steadied myself. It was nice to know which way was up, finally. I thought about just hanging around until the power came back on, but who's to say it even would? I put one palm against the wall, feeling for vibrations. I'd been on this station long enough to know what it should normally feel like. I could feel a faint thrumming, which was probably the life support system. Good. At least we weren't going to run out of air. But that also showed me the extent of the damage.

Warpside Station had two backup systems. Backup One came on if the station lost power, and it kept the oxygen going as well as the artificial gravity and temperature control. Backup Two only came on if Backup One failed, and it only did the bare minimum to keep the occupants alive. Since the gravity was out, we had to be on Backup Two. What could have damaged the primary systems as well as Backup One?

I needed to get to the lowest level ASAP. But I'd need some tools and a light source. Clothing would have been nice too. But first I'd need to get out of this room. I wasn't sure which wall I was on, but I knew the shower heads were evenly placed around all four walls. The nozzles were about two meters apart, which was a bit out of my reach. But with such a clear picture of the layout in my head, I knew I could make it around the room if I was careful. I visualized where the next nozzle was, and launched myself towards it.

I caught the next nozzle, steadied myself, got my bearings, and launched myself again. Using this method, I felt my way around the room, navigated the corner, and kept going. Finally I found a doorway. I wasn't sure if it was the one that led to the locker room or the restroom, but I pushed it open and climbed through.

I was still blind, but this room was narrower and had a

much lower ceiling, making it much easier to navigate. There was a bench running along the middle of the room, on which I stubbed my already-injured toe as I floated from one wall to the other. I hit the lockers with a hollow clang. Definitely the locker room, then. Good. I knew my clothing was in one of them, but even if I somehow found the right locker in the dark, I wouldn't be able to open the electronic lock with the power out.

Still, the lockers weren't completely useless. Each one had a handle, giving me lots of things to grab as I half-walked, half-floated to the other side of the room. On reaching the far wall, I felt around until I found the door. This one couldn't simply be pushed open. It was a powered hatch, designed to open automatically when someone approached. But it did have a manual handle for emergencies. I felt around until I found a recessed groove, and holding onto another part of the door for leverage, I pulled the handle. The door popped open a few centimeters, and I pried it the rest of the way.

A short, L-shaped hallway led to the gym. Well, I say "gym," but it was actually more of a recreation center and tourist trap. The huge round room was designed to look like a park. It had video screens around the perimeter that usually displayed images of a forest, making the gym look even larger than it was. A jogging path ran along the outer wall. Other activities included climbing walls and rope walks and such. Even the traditional gym equipment, like the weights and exercise bikes, were designed to fit the forest motif.

Of course, I couldn't see any of that right then, as everything was still pitch black. I kept one hand on the hallway exit, and tried to visualize the gym. I was tempted to just push off the wall and float to the other side, but I knew there were so many obstacles on the way, that I was afraid I'd get turned around. The ceiling was even higher here than in the showers. The last thing I wanted was to be up near the ceiling when the gravity came back on.

If it came back on.

I remembered some benches near the locker rooms. They were as good a place as any to start. I pictured them in my mind, put one foot against the wall behind me, and gently pushed myself forward. I free-floated through the darkness once again, my arms straight ahead of me, ready to grab the bench when I reached it. But I'd gone too high, and I banged my knee on the bench instead. "Damn!" I shouted. I quickly grabbed the bench before it was out of reach, and hugged it.

"Is someone there?" It was a woman's voice. It didn't sound very close by.

"Yes!" I shouted. "Where are you?"

"I think I'm under the treehouse thingie," she said. "I'm holding onto the rope wall."

I knew where it was. There was a wooden fort near the middle of the room, which you accessed by climbing a big rope spiderweb. It was mostly there for kids, but I'd climbed it more than a few times in the past. "I'll be right there," I said. I had a pretty good idea which direction I needed to go. I positioned myself so that I could push off from the bench with my legs, and leaped.

I floated for several seconds, arms once again outstretched. Then my foot hit something metal, I'm still not sure what, and I started tumbling head over heels. After a few more seconds I crashed into what felt like an elliptical machine. "Ow!" I shouted.

"Are you okay?" the woman asked.

"Yeah, just give me a minute." I was completely turned around, but I centered on her voice again, and used the exercise machine to launch myself in that direction. I Marco Polo'ed my way around the room for another few minutes, crashed a couple more times, and eventually landed in the spiderweb. My forearm smacked the mysterious woman right across the face.

"Sorry," I said.

"It's fine," she said. "It sounded like you got a few bruises of your own getting over here."

"I'm Jil," I said, hooking a leg and an elbow through the spiderweb so I wouldn't float away.

"Vee," she said. "Any idea what's going on?"

"Not a clue," I said. "I was in the showers when it happened."

"I was here," Vee said. "The sign said the gym was closed for maintenance, but I went in anyway. I just wanted to look around, I wasn't going to hurt anything. When the lights went out, for a second I thought it was my fault. Like an alarm or something."

"I doubt it's anything you did," I said.

"Does this happen a lot?"

"The power flickers sometimes, but I've never seen *this* happen," I said.

"You live here on the station?" she asked.

"Yep, I'm a local."

"So what happens now?" she asked. "Do we just wait here for the power to come back on?"

"Well... that depends on what's wrong," I said. "And I really should get down to the engine rooms and find out."

"Not without me, you don't," she said.

"I'm not really allowed to bring visitors down there," I said. "You know, machinery, danger, lawsuits."

"You're the first person I've seen since the power went out," she said.

"Technically you haven't—"

"You know what I mean," Vee said. "You're not leaving me here alone."

"Okay, okay," I said. "You can come. Just promise me you won't sue if something goes wrong."

"Deal," she said. "Shake on it?" I could feel the ropes vibrate as she moved one of her hands.

"That's... not my hand," I said.

"Oh!" she said, pulling her hand away. "Right, you said you were showering. Sorry. Do you want some clothes?"

"You have some to spare?"

"Give me a second," she said, and the rope web started shaking a lot. After a few seconds she handed me something with sleeves. A jacket. I put it on. The ropes continued to shake, and then she handed me some pants.

"You were wearing two pairs of pants?" I asked.

"No, but it's okay," she said. "I've got boxers on."

"Thanks," I said. "I don't suppose you have a flashlight?"

"Can't help you there," she answered.

"Well, there should be one in the toolkit downstairs," I said. "We'll have to find our way to the maintenance shafts, but I know those tunnels like the back of my hand."

"What if we get separated?"

"Just hang onto me," I said. "Though we could use this rope. If I only had a knife…"

"Inside jacket pocket," Vee said.

I felt around and found a small pocket knife. I cut a long length of rope off of the spiderweb, and we each tied one end around our waist.

Now secured to each other, we worked our way back to the gym's outer wall. We made a few missteps along the way, and most of them were my fault, to be honest. She seemed to be more comfortable with zero-G maneuvers than I was. We reached the gym's door with no major injuries. Unfortunately, it wouldn't open. We found the emergency release hatch, but the door still wouldn't pop.

"That's not good," I said.

"Shouldn't the emergency release always work?" Vee asked.

"Something's engaged the deadbolt system," I told her. I waited to see if she asked what that was, but she just made an affirmative sound. Some key doors around the station had extra locks that only engaged in specific emergencies, such as a hull breach or a virus outbreak. This prevented panicking visitors from opening doors that needed to stay sealed, to keep the problem from spreading throughout the station.

"Does this mean there's no air outside the gym?" Vee asked.

I shook my head, not that she could see it. "Whatever happened, happened fast," I said. "There were no announcements. But the deadbolts can only engage during Backup One, not Two. Someone had to take us to B-One, engage the deadbolts, then advance to B-Two, without sounding any alarms. At the very least, there's supposed to be an automatic, station-wide klaxon that sounds when B-One activates."

"What are you thinking?" Vee asked.

"Seems too complex to be an accident," I said. "I'm pretty sure the station's been hacked."

She paused for a few seconds before she spoke. "Pirates?" she asked.

"Could be," I said. It wasn't uncommon for pirates to use computer viruses to shut down ships and space stations. But pirates didn't usually operate so close to a warp gate, where police could arrive at any moment. Still, it was the best theory we had.

"They're not going to raid the gym," Vee said. "There's nothing to steal in here. If we wait here 'til they're done stealing whatever they came for, the power will come back on, and we'll be safe. Right?"

"Depends on the pirates," I said. "Some of them have a sense of honor. And some of them are just as likely to shut down the rest of the life support on their way out, just so there's fewer witnesses."

I heard her take a deep breath. "So what do we do now?" she asked.

I thought for a minute. I pictured the layout of the gym, as well as all the exits and surrounding crawlways. There were several utility hatches in the gym, some of which would lead to the maintenance tunnels. Unfortunately they couldn't be opened without power, at least not from the outside. But there was one with an outer latch... It hadn't occurred to me before because it was usually inaccessible.

There was a large access hatch in the center of the gym's ceiling. I'd only seen it used a couple of times, to lower new exercise equipment from the hotel level to the gym. And since it was usually out of reach, it wouldn't have deadbolts. Maybe.

"I hope you're not afraid of heights," I said. It was a silly joke, given the situation, but she laughed anyway. I liked her laugh. *Don't get distracted*, I told myself. For all I knew, she had three husbands.

Finding the hatch wasn't too difficult. The ceiling curved towards the center, and there were several pipes and other handholds to grab onto. The hatch's handle was tight from lack of use, but working together, we managed to get it open.

The tunnel had a low ceiling. We'd have had to crouch if we'd been walking. But since there was no gravity, we just climbed along the walls, using inertia to float forward, keeping our hands above our heads to keep from slamming into anything.

After a few minutes we heard some banging noises above us. I grabbed a utility pipe to stop myself, and asked Vee to stop as well. She moved until she was by my side, and we held hands to keep from drifting away. Even though our bodies were technically horizontal, it felt like we were standing next to each other. "Did you hear that?" I asked.

"What's above us?" she asked.

"Hotel rooms, I imagine," I said. "Probably guests trapped in their rooms. They've got to be freaking out."

"Can we reach any of them?" Vee asked. "Maybe one has a flashlight or something."

"Or a comm unit," I added. "Even if they've blocked communications, we could still use some of the apps right now. I've got a night vision app on mine. Say, where's yours?"

"Back in my room," she said. "I didn't want to take it to the gym. Of course, I didn't know the gym would be closed. I wouldn't have even gone in, but there was this creepy guy in the lobby, and I didn't want to wait for the lift again with him around."

"What did he look like?" I asked.

"Human, pale skin, dark hair in a ponytail, wearing a janitor's outfit. Oh, and he had sunglasses on. Know him?"

"Doesn't sound familiar," I said. It was weird. I mean, I thought I knew all the janitors. But I had to put that on the back burner for now. "Well, there aren't any hatches that lead directly to hotel rooms. There was one directly above the hatch to the gym, but it would probably be locked. And there might be pirates walking around up there. I think we should stick with the original plan."

She agreed, and we continued on our way. We finally came to a vertical shaft, which had an actual ladder. We climbed into the shaft and headed downwards, head first. Climbing up just felt more intuitive than climbing down, even though we were headed for the lower levels. Along the way, we talked about our jobs. When Vee told me the name of the delivery company she worked for, I did a double-take.

"Oh!" I said, laughing. "You're that cute girl who stole my chicken!"

"I thought you sounded familiar," Vee said. "If we get out of this, I'll buy you a steak dinner."

"Deal," I said. "Shake on it?" We both laughed.

It was slow going because I didn't want to lose track of where we were. Every few rungs I'd reach out and make sure I could still feel the nearby walls, so we wouldn't pass right by the next junction without noticing. We reached the bottom – or top, depending on your point of view – of the gym level, passed the junction, and began climbing past the crew quarters. We passed another junction, and finally reached the engine level.

I'd spent more time on that floor than I had in my own quarters, and I knew my way around pretty well. I found a hatch with no problem, popped it, and felt my way around a corner. There was an unlocked storage locker a few meters in, and I knew I'd find a flashlight inside. But as soon as I touched it, I heard a man's voice. "Hey you!" he shouted. I barely had time to figure out which direction the voice had come from, when he slammed into me.

Fighting in zero-G is weird. With every punch, you risk propelling yourself backward, so it's hard to stay near your opponent. But this guy knew what he was doing. He held onto my jacket with one hand, and threw punches with the other. By the accuracy of his fists, I could tell he was able to see me. I managed to block a few hits with my hands, but I knew I wasn't going to last long at this rate.

Then he made an "Urk!" sound, and took his hands off me. I didn't waste the opportunity. Using the same strategy he'd just shown me, I grabbed his clothing with one hand and wailed on him with the other. My job keeps me pretty fit, and I can hit hard for someone my size.

"It's okay, I think he's out," Vee said. I heard her fumbling with something. There was a faint sound like rattling plastic. "Oh, wow," she said.

"What is it?" I asked.

"Here," she said. "Put these on for a sec."

I held my hand out, and she placed something in them. Sunglasses. I put them on, and suddenly I could see again. It wasn't full color, but a thousand shades of green. There was also a bit of a lag whenever I turned my head. But after spending the last hour or so in total darkness, it was amazing. I looked at my attacker. Vee had taken the rope tied between us, and wrapped it around his neck. He looked like the man she'd described earlier, with the ponytail and the janitor outfit.

I looked up at Vee. "Those aren't boxers," I said.

"I was hoping we'd be back in our own clothes before the lights came back on," she said, covering up her skimpy underwear.

"I can fix that right now," I said. Working together, we

stripped the imposter down to his underclothes. I gave Vee back her jacket and pants, then put on the janitor outfit. I had to untie the rope from around my waist to do so, but there were plenty of things to hold onto. The one-piece jumpsuit was a little large on me, but I'd live. He'd also been wearing a pair of magnetic boots. I put them on, and was able to walk on the floor once again.

Now that I could see, I got my toolbox out of the locker. There were two head-mounted flashlights, so I gave one to Vee. I had to take the glasses off, as using them with the flashlight made everything too bright.

"What should we do with his guy?" I asked, looking back at the pirate who'd jumped me. He was breathing, but out cold.

Now that we had the lights, we decided that we wouldn't need to be tethered together. So we used the rope to tie the pirate to some pipes. Vee kept glancing at me while I tightened the knots. Her face was full of concern. "Are you okay?" she finally asked.

I touched my face, and it came away bloody. Odd. I'd seen a couple of drops of blood float past my face, but I'd assumed they were from the pirate. Vee spotted a first aid kit on the wall, and jumped over to it. Watching her move, I could tell this wasn't the first time she'd been in a zero-G crisis. I couldn't wait for that dinner she'd promised, so I could ask her about her past adventures.

Vee doted on me for a few minutes, dabbing something on my face with a cotton ball. She had to be careful with the liquid due to the lack of gravity, but once again I got the impression that she'd done this before. Just who was this woman?

Whatever the topical medicine was, it worked wonders. I hadn't realized how much pain I was in until I felt it fade away. Vee held onto the first aid kit in case we needed it again, and I went through our captive's things. There were a couple of pouches on his belt, in which I found a two-way communicator and a small hacking device. He didn't have any weapons, but that wasn't surprising. The station's scanners were quite good at screening for firearms.

"Come on," I said, leading Vee around the corner. We had to manually open another hatch, which let us into the engine control room. Most of the terminals were off, but two still hummed faintly with activity: Life Support and Master Controls. I walked over to the MC computer. Vee held onto my shoulder, floating gently in mid-air.

"Can you turn the power back on?" she asked.

"Probably," I replied, turning the pirate's hacking device over and over in my hands. "But I'm not sure if it's a great idea. Let's see what the situation is first."

The controls were locked out. The pirates had even changed the master override password. But sticking the hacking device into the computer's input port gave me complete control over the system. First I called up the activity log to see what had happened so far. From what I could gather, the pirates had docked in a nondescript transport ship, then integrated into the crew using fake IDs and uniforms. Once they were in position, our janitor friend had hacked the master controls. Then they'd taken advantage of the chaos, using magnetic boots and darkvision glasses.

From this computer, the fake janitor could restore power to specific sections at a time, just long enough to open or lock key doors. From what I could tell, the pirates had been sweeping the station, one room at a time. Communications were blocked. The station was currently sending out an automatic signal warning other ships to stay away, due to a potential virus outbreak.

I restored power to the security cameras, and checked the video feed. Most of them just showed pitch-black rooms. However, two rooms were well-lit. One of the shops on the top floor was currently being picked apart, the pirates loading every bit of merchandise onto hovering carts. On the hotel level, the hallway light was on, and one of the hotel room doors was open. As I watched, four pirates harassed a pair of hotel guests, stripping them and taking their valuables. When the pirates were satisfied that they'd taken everything the couple had to offer, they ordered them back into their room. Then one pulled out their communicator.

I jumped as the communicator in my pouch spoke. "Jakeb. Lock H thirty-two, unlock H thirty-three." I froze, not sure if I should respond. Then the voice came again. "Jakeb! You napping or what?"

I hurriedly tapped a few keys. On the monitor, One room door closed and locked, and the next room opened. The pirates rushed into the new room and pulled the occupants into the hall.

Vee looked up from the monitor and gave me an incredulous look. "You're helping them?"

"No," I said. "Just buying us a minute while I think."

"Just call the police or something," she said.

"Done," I said, sending a signal to the IGP. But I was afraid it wasn't enough. The pirates looked like they were almost done, and might be long gone before the police arrived. Then I had a thought.

"What are you doing?" Vee asked, as I tapped through menus and submenus, looking for the right commands.

"Giving them a taste of their own medicine," I said. Then I reactivated the station-wide PA system. "This is the InterGalactic Police. We have detected pirate activity aboard Warpside Station. Stay where you are, and prepare to be captured." The words echoed throughout the station.

On the video screen, I watched as the pirates dropped whatever they were holding and scrambled to get back to their ship. Some used their magnetic boots to run, but it was slow going, and they kept tripping over their own feet trying to run faster. Others turned off their boots, jumping off the walls as they flew down the hallways. The communicator spoke again. "Jakeb. Turn the power back on and get to the ship."

I clicked on the communicator. "This is Officer Peet. I'm afraid Jakeb is already in custody," I said.

Vee and I laughed as we watched the pirates crawl over each other, pushing their fellow criminals into walls to get to the ship first. Once the majority of the pirates were onboard their ship, they sealed the doors and attempted to take off. However, they ran into a problem.

When a ship docks at Warpside Station, their computer systems are patched into ours. This allows us to perform some maintenance operations while the guests enjoy our hospitality. This doesn't usually give us complete control over their ship. Jakeb's hacking device, however, was synced to their ship's computer, allowing me to take over their systems.

I shut down their power, their gravity, everything but their life support. I also locked all their hatches, turning their ship into a prison. When the police finally arrived, they were like fish in a barrel.

Later that night, Vee made good on her promise. Over a fantastic steak dinner at the mall's only posh restaurant, we talked for hours. She told me about how she played a lot of G-ball in her youth, a sport that required a lot of moving around in zero-G. I told her all about my passion for fixing machinery, and she listened with great interest. She said she was saving up for her own delivery ship someday, and offered me a job as her ship's mechanic. It was a beautiful thought, the two of us making our way through the universe together, but it was a far-off dream.

Vee told me she'd have to leave the following morning to stay on her shipping schedule, but she promised she'd come see me every time she passed through this warp gate. And since she had some degree of control over which jobs she accepted, she agreed to take more jobs on this route. For my part, I promised I would make time for her visits, switching shifts when possible if I knew she was coming.

We had a deal. After dinner, I took her back to my room so we could shake on it.

Vigilante

Ember leaned on the rail of the fire escape of her second-story apartment, overlooking the poorest part of town. The moon was just a sliver in the sky, and half the streetlamps were out, but she could still make out the customers trickling in and out of the bar across the street. Their laughter echoed up from below, sounding eerie and ghostlike by the time they reached Ember's ears.

But then a new sound joined in. It was faint, but she heard shrieking from her right. She strained her eyes for the source. She could just make out three stick figures running through an empty lot. As her eyes adjusted, she saw that it was a young woman being pursued by two men. Ember reached into her pocket and pulled out her cell phone. She was about to call the police, but she knew they'd never arrive in time. The response time in her neighborhood was notoriously lax.

She briefly considered running down to help, but fear took over. She knew she'd just become a victim herself. She'd been brave once, but that was before her egg had cracked, before she'd started living as her true self. Since then she'd been a bully magnet, and she'd yet to win a fight against the transphobic bigots that roamed her street. If she went down there now, she probably wouldn't make it back home.

She looked at her phone again, and pressed the

"Emergency Call" button. Maybe it was futile, but she had to do *something*. But while she waited for an operator to pick up, a fourth figure joined the group. Another feminine shape, dressed in black like a ninja, with a long ponytail trailing from her mask. She got between the men and their intended victim, then taunted them, goading them into a fight.

One of the guys ran right up to her, and she kicked him in the chin. As he went down, the other man tried to attack her from the side, and she punched him. The second guy staggered back for a second, then lunged forward. The dark woman then did something Ember couldn't really see. It looked like she just touched him on the forehead with her index finger. Whatever it was, the guy immediately fell flat on his back. The first guy started to get back up, only to get kicked again. He stayed down this time.

The intended victim had wedged herself behind a trash can, and now her rescuer helped her get to her feet. It looked like they said a few words to each other, then the ninja woman ran back into the darkness.

"Emergency Services, how may I direct your call?"

Oh. Ember had forgotten she was holding the phone. "I'm… not sure," Ember said, staring off into the darkness.

"So, I was patrolling the neighborhood, like I do most nights. And I heard a scream. Not a 'bloody murder' scream, more of a desperate protest."

"What was it?"

"I tuned my directional microphone until I heard it again. It was coming from a parking lot. Three guys were harassing a young woman. Half of her clothing lay on the ground, ripped. The men were calling her an 'effing whore' and beating her badly. One of them was undoing his pants."

"So you stopped them."

"What else could I do? They were going to rape her, and probably kill her."

"Were you afraid?"

"If I'd stopped to think about it, I might have been. But I just jumped in. I had the element of surprise."

"But you were outnumbered. And they were stronger, right?"

"Well, yes. But I know karate."

"This isn't a movie. You didn't stop three strong men using karate."

"Well, no..."

"I'm just afraid that this might be another way of attempting suicide."

"Then why would I fight back?"

"Maybe you're afraid suicide would make your life meaningless. Maybe you want to die a hero."

"Look, I didn't want to fight them. I just wanted her to be safe. And there wasn't time to call the police."

"Okay, so you 'heroically leaped into the fray.' Maybe not the best decision, but then I'm not you. Then what happened?"

"I yelled for the woman to run. Then I fought them."

"You obviously survived. So you managed to take them out, all by yourself?"

"Not exactly. I got one of them down using my taser gloves, and I managed to mace another one. But the third one blindsided me. I nearly bought it."

"How did you escape?"

"The victim - she didn't run after all. She hit one of the attackers with a board."

"I see."

"And then they were down. We'd won. I'd saved a life. Then I stood over one of the attackers... and... and... I picked up his knife. And I wondered what kind of person could do such a thing to another human being. Here was someone who was willing to destroy another person's life, just for a few minutes of pleasure. I held the knife tightly, and I could see myself swipe it across his throat."

"You didn't."

"It wasn't easy to stop myself. I mean, what he was about to do to that girl - I really wanted to just kill him right there."

"But you *did* stop yourself."

"Of course. But even so, I could just see myself giving in. The world simply doesn't need someone like that in it."

"So what stopped you?"

"I was... afraid."

"Of?"

"If I took that step, what else would I be capable of? My identity... You know I'm changing. I don't know everything about the person I'm becoming, but I know who I don't want to be."

"So what did you do?"

"I tasered the guy one more time for good measure, and threw the knife in the dumpster. I told the woman to go somewhere safe and call the police. And then I went home."

"Good. Dan, you know you're an unusual patient. You saved my life once. And for that reason alone, I'm giving you more leeway than I would most patients. But if I ever decide that you're a threat to yourself or society at large, I'm turning you in."

"Doc, I wouldn't have it any other way."

"Well, we still have a few minutes left. Would you like to discuss your gender issues?"

Danielle made sure no one could see her, and took off her mask. Then she retrieved her overcoat from where she'd stuffed it behind the trash bin. The coat smelled like garbage – again – but at least no one would see her walking around in her superhero costume. She crossed the street and took the stairs up to her apartment.

Once inside, she threw her overcoat into the laundry hamper and removed her body armor. First, her taser-fingered gloves. Then her heavy combat boots. Her molded plastic vest came off next, and then her black bodysuit. Finally, she removed her underwear and threw it in with the laundry. On the way to the shower, she looked in the mirror and sighed.

As usual, Daniel stared back at her. As men went, he wasn't bad looking. He was a little on the short side, but he had a clean face and a swimmer's body. Danielle didn't hate Daniel. But she longed for the day when she could look in the mirror and see Danielle.

If that day ever came. She hadn't even started taking hormones yet. There was no way her job would let her transition. Sure, she could try to sue them if they fired her, but they'd just claim they'd fired her for some other reason. And she was lucky to have a decent job, with unemployment on the rise. Of course, even with her job, her paychecks didn't stretch much past the bills.

She could either live as Daniel or starve as Danielle. Those were her only two choices.

Ember ran through the alley, knocking over trash cans as she went. The three men were still behind her. She'd been clocked on the way home from work, and these guys weren't playing around. Ember had become something of a connoisseur of bullies lately. Some of them just wanted to feel powerful, some wanted to impress their friends, and some of them just liked the chase.

But these guys were motivated by blind hatred. Who knew why – maybe they were religious zealots, or maybe they just hated their own lives so much that they had to take it out on someone else. Hell, maybe they'd been bitten by a trans person when they were kids. Regardless of the reason, they weren't playing around. Ember had no doubt that if they caught her, they'd kill her.

She tried to run somewhere where there might be witnesses, but they were so close behind her that she couldn't even take the time to think. It was all react, react,

react. As she turned another corner, she belatedly realized that she was in the alley behind her own apartment. She'd subconsciously run home, her panicked brain associating it with safety. *Idiot!* she admonished herself. She couldn't let them see where she lived.

That last thought had her second-guess her next steps, and she tripped over her own feet. With her pursuers standing right behind her, she just curled into a ball, closed her eyes, and waited for the kicking to begin.

But the kicks never came. "Who the hell is that?" one of the bullies asked.

"Get out of here while you can still walk," another said.

But whoever they were talking to, no answer was forthcoming. Instead she heard sounds of fighting, the clattering of garbage cans, and several cries of pain. When Ember dared to open her eyes, she saw one of her attackers limping away, the other two unconscious on the ground. And that ninja woman was standing over her, offering her a hand.

Ember took it, but immediately realized something felt wrong. The ninja's hand was slippery, and when Ember jerked her hand away, she saw that it was covered in blood. A huge gash ran along her savior's side, and she was teetering, about to collapse.

"Let me help you," Ember said, getting to her feet. "I live just up there." She threw the ninja's arm over her shoulder, and together they made it up the stairs to Ember's apartment.

"You're lucky I'm a nursing student," a voice said, as Danielle slowly regained consciousness. She remembered fighting some jerks in an alley, but then, that could have described any night this week.

"Where am I?" Danielle asked. She could tell she was in a bed, but it didn't feel like her own.

"My place," Ember answered.

Danielle opened her eyes, blinked a few times, and looked around. It was a small apartment, with old fixtures and painted brick walls. She searched the room until her eyes found Ember. When she saw her face, it all came back to her. The chase, the victim, the alley, the fight.

"Are you okay?" Danielle asked.

"Better than you," Ember said, walking over. "You were stabbed three times. This one was pretty deep." She pulled down the blanket and pointed to the bandage along Danielle's side.

Danielle realized she was naked, and pulled the blanket back up.

Ember laughed. "Don't worry, I'm practically a nurse. I would have taken you to the hospital, but somehow I had the feeling you wouldn't like that."

Danielle shook her head. "Thanks," she said. "That might not have gone well for me."

"Can I ask you a stupid question?" Ember asked. "Actually, several."

"Go ahead," Danielle said.

"The chest piece? The ponytail?"

"It's not some fetish if that's what you're asking," Danielle replied. "I just like the look. I feel more like myself that way. You wouldn't understand."

"You might be surprised," Ember said. "Next question. Do you just have a death wish or something? I mean, thank you, seriously, thank you, but you're going to get yourself killed. I saw you the other night too, saving another girl. You're doing good work, I mean that. But I almost ran off last night, once I was safe. If I hadn't helped you, you would have bled out."

Danielle waved her off. "I know," she said. "And I don't know. This city has gotten out of control, and the police refuse to do a damn thing. There are rapes and murders every night. Gang activity is everywhere. It just makes me so furious. I had to do something."

"Well, you're brave, I'll give you that," Ember said. "And I wish more people were like you. But sooner or later you're going to get shot, or stabbed again, or beaten to death."

Danielle's expression made Ember go pale. She knew that look, because she'd seen it in the mirror herself. It was a look that said, *Would that be so bad?*

Ember's heart melted, and she sat down on the bed, putting a hand on Danielle's shoulder. "You want to die a hero," Ember said.

"It's all I've got left," Danielle said. "I can't transition and work where I do. I can't find another job that pays a living wage. I can't afford HRT or surgeries. I can't afford to move to another city, and I'd feel like a traitor if I did. Like I was abandoning the city's other victims to their fates."

"Have you talked to anyone?" Ember asked. "Like a therapist?"

"I have a psychologist," Danielle said. "That's at least covered by my insurance. But it won't pay for anything transition-related. I feel so trapped, locked in by circumstances. I'm living in a cage, and the key is just beyond my reach. I can't make more money, I can't find more opportunities, and I can't be my true self. All I'm left with is anger, and if I'm going to lash out, I might as well take it out on people who deserve it."

Ember nodded. "If you're going to die anyway, might as well hurt some bad people on the way," she said. She didn't agree with the statement, she was just finishing Danielle's thought.

Danielle considered her words, then quietly said, "Exactly."

"What's your name?" Ember asked.

"Danielle."

Ember looked at her. The person in her bed looked like a man, with a svelte but muscular frame, and close-cropped hair. But if she wanted to be seen as a woman, Ember was the last person who would judge her. At least, not for that.

"Danielle," Ember said. "You're a fool."

"Huh?"

"First off, have you considered all the other possible outcomes of your activities? Sure, maybe you'll die a hero. But you're just as likely to end up in jail or in a wheelchair, neither of which is going to make your life any peachier. You think it's hard to get a decent job now, just wait until you have a criminal record. Or when you're missing a limb."

Danielle looked like she was about to object, but Ember kept going.

"And secondly, I know you think that going out in a blaze of glory is 'dying on your own terms' or 'taking control of your life' or whatever, but it's not. It's just another way of letting the bad guys win. You said you didn't want move away because, what was it, you didn't want to betray the other victims?"

"Something like that," Danielle said softly. "I'd be abandoning them."

"Well, it's the same if you die. You'd be leaving behind thousands of other trans people, like myself. We're stronger together, and any loss weakens us all. We need your voice and your votes if we're ever going to make the world safer for all of us."

They were both quiet for a minute. Finally, Danielle said, "Then I'm back to square one."

"No," Ember said, taking Danielle's hands into hers. "You're better off than you were yesterday, because now you have a friend."

Danielle looked into her eyes, lost in thought. She'd always pictured her life as a comic book, with a poverty-stricken backstory leading to years of heroic fights and daring rescues, culminating in a hero's fall that would inspire others to keep up the good fight. But maybe this wasn't that story. Maybe this wasn't a comic book at all, but an inspirational story about someone who almost made a terrible mistake, only to be rescued by someone else.

And maybe the climax wouldn't be as flashy as the comic book would have been. Gone was the iconic cover where another hero carried Danielle's limp form away from the alien battlefield, with a splash of text declaring, "In This Issue – A Hero Falls!" In its place, Danielle pictured a photo album, gradually growing over the years, filled with happy moments with her new friend.

Exciting? No. A best-seller? Definitely not. But a better ending? That was the question. Staring into Ember's beautiful eyes, Danielle found her answer.

They moved in together two months later. As roommates, they faced fewer expenses, and were able to save a bit more. Ember eventually became a full-time nurse, and Danielle's search for a better job finally paid off. Within a year, Danielle started living as a woman full-time. A few years later, Ember and Danielle were married.

And Danielle never put on the mask again.

Author's Notes

Spoilers ahead!

Growing up, romance was one of those genres I just didn't "get." For the longest time, I thought I hated love stories. But a few years after my egg cracked, I happened to see a lesbian romance novel on sale, and the plot was just interesting enough to turn my head. And I was hooked. It turns out I do like romance after all, I just find straight couples boring.

But that's not why I wrote this. This little collection is, to be perfectly honest, stories that didn't fit anywhere else. When I wrote my Bloodhunters series, I threw in every idea I had, sometimes shoving square pegs into round holes just to make them fit the universe. Sometimes it worked, and sometimes it didn't.

A woman who keeps reincarnating with the same initials? Why not. A planet full of warring cat and dog people? I'll make it fit. A medieval world whose residents don't know they're being watched by the rest of the universe? Okay, I'll work it in somewhere. I'll be the first to admit that some of these ideas would have been better off in their own universes.

The stories in this collection are the ones that I simply couldn't fit in the Bloodhunters universe. Some because they involve magic and mysticism, others because they just worked better set in modern day. Some of these stories are based on fantasies of mine, of people I wish I could be.

Dungeon Therapy

I thought of the basic concept back in the 90s, but the plot didn't have legs until COVID came along. I spent a good deal of the pandemic playing RPGs with my friends over the internet, and we faced some of the same challenges. In a weird way, Dot is an author avatar. As a non-transitioning trans woman, I often feel like hiding my face from the world, and living my life online.

Gilded Cage

Originally this was going to be Romeo & Juliet with drones. That gradually morphed into something closer to Rapunzel. The ending surprised me a little. Of course I meant for the two characters to end up together, but as I was writing it, their chemistry seemed a little off. Rather than fine tune their interactions, I decided to give it an ending that felt more natural to me.

Mother's Day

Sometimes when I get up in the middle of the night to use the restroom, I have visions of some monstrous, lanky thing crawling up the stairs. The image stuck with me long enough that I pretty much had to write it down. Btw, everything I know about police procedure, I learned from television, so I'm sure I got everything right. (Sarcasm sign.)

Fairy Dust

I wrote the first half of this one in the early 2000s, to go along with an online RPG module I was hosting. The server was called "Fairies vs Dragons," and it was exactly what it said on the tin. Players could choose to be either of the two species, with multiple subspecies options, and fight each other in PvP areas.

* * *

Hero Worship

My favorite part of any superhero story is when someone finds out their secret identity. Originally this story started with someone finding a superhero's purse in an alley, where the hero had changed before they went off to fight crime. The finished story turned out so different, that you could probably steal the above idea without me getting too mad at you.

Think Tank

This story started as wish fulfillment, something I started thinking about right after a certain president was elected. I was so disappointed at the voters at the time, I had daydreams about Jesus returning to Earth to clarify a few things. Which is weird, because I'm an atheist.

The actual speech went through a ton of changes, and I'm still not satisfied with how it came out. The final version is a bit of an author tract, but the earlier versions were even longer and preachier.

Strangers in the Void

This takes place in the same universe as my Bloodhunters series, but I don't know when or where. Nitpickers will probably find all sorts of problems with the science, but hey, look, a squirrel!

The first time I ever experienced total darkness was in a friend's basement. I was probably around eight or ten, and I thought I knew what pitch black looked like. I mean, who doesn't know what darkness looks like? But the truth is, total darkness is oddly rare, especially in the modern age. Between the moon, stars, fireflies, digital clocks, phones, street lamps, headlights, business signs and other light pollution, we're rarely completely in the dark. And even when we are, we can trust our other senses to keep us grounded. The idea of free-floating in total darkness terrifies me.

Vigilante

Originally I envisioned this as a comic book series, about a trans woman who lived as a man by day, but had a female superhero persona. Of course, in the years since I thought up with the concept, there have been a few transgender superheros in both comics and on TV. Still, it sounded like a fun concept, so I dusted off my old notes and started writing it out as a short story.

It was originally going to be called "T-Girl" with the "T" officially standing for taser (wink wink). But the more I typed, the more ridiculous it sounded. I'm not a huge fan of deconstruction, but when you really think about it, it's hard to write realistic superheroes. The very concept is so full of idealism and wishful thinking, that you have to assume certain realities just don't exist in your universe.

If I'd carried on as planned, Ember would have become Danielle's "gal in the chair," stitching the hero up after every battle. But when it came time for Danielle to actually justify her lifestyle to Ember, I just couldn't do it. Because it's dumb. So rather than this story telling the origin of a hero as planned, it tells why one retires. The ending might be a little flat compared to the original plan, but in its own way, I think it's uplifting.

I hope you enjoyed these stories. If you like my writing style, be sure to check out my other books. And don't forget to leave reviews, tell your friends, and follow me on social media. Thanks for reading!

Special thanks to my beta readers, KJ and Kaius.

About the Author

Xine Fury has 206 bones and is made up of 60% water.

The following books by Xine Fury are also available:
    Bloodhunters v1: Bad Blood
    Bloodhunters v2: Blue Blood
    Bloodhunters v3: New Blood
    Blood Samples (A Bloodhunters Prequel)
    Rainbow Nightmares
    Gender Rolls
    Side Quests
    Nomads of Zyden

Find them here: bit.ly/XineFury